I'm Waiting for You
STORIES TO GIVE YOU HOPE

By Adela M Robinson

I'm Waiting For You

Copyright @ 2024 Adela M Robinson

The right of Adela M Robinson to be identified as the Author of the work has been asserted by her in accordance with the Copyright Designs and Patents Act 1988. No part of this book may be reproduced in any form to photocopying or by any electronic or mechanical means, including information storage or retrieval systems without permission in writing from both the copyright owner and the publisher of this book.

This work is fiction. Names and characters are the product of the author's imagination.

Cover Design by Gemma Curran
ISBN: 9798391409458
First Published in 2024 by Amazon Kindle Direct Publishing

Scripture quotations marked (TLB) are taken from The Living Bible, copyright @ 1971 by Tyndale House Foundation. Used by permission of Tyndale House Publishers, Carol Stream, Illinois 60188. All rights reserved.

Scripture quotations marked (NIV) are taken from the Holy Bible, New International Version®, NIV®. Copyright @ 1973, 1978, 1984, 2011 by Biblica, Inc.™ Used by permission of Zondervan. All rights reserved worldwide. www.zondervan.com The "NIV" and "New International Version" are trademarks registered in the United States Patent and Trademark Office by Biblica, Inc.™

Scripture quotations marked (NKJV) taken from the New King James Version®. Copyright @ 1982 by Thomas Nelson. Used by permission. All rights reserved.

Scripture quotations marked (NLT) are taken from the Holy Bible, New Living Translation, copyright @1996, 2004, 2015 by Tyndale House Foundation. Used by permission of Tyndale House Publishers, Carol Stream, Illinois 60188. All rights reserved.

Scripture quotations marked (GNT) are from the Good News Translation in Today's English Version- Second Edition Copyright @ 1992 by American Bible Society. Used by Permission.

Scripture quotations marked (NASB) taken from the New American Standard Bible®, Copyright @ 1960, 1971, 1977, 1995, 2020 by The Lockman Foundation. Used by permission. All rights reserved. lockman.org

CONTENTS

Introduction
Acknowledgement
The Kiss   3
A Second Chance   22
The Watch   40
I'm Waiting for You   68
Never Too Late   88
The Telephone Call   123
Pray without Ceasing   142
The Wedding Gown   175
The Honeymoon   191
Epilogue: The Nail   224

INTRODUCTION

You're about to be awe-inspired, strengthened, and acquire knowledge of your own self-worth and how much God loves you.

My joy and passion is to see women motivated and encouraged to live out their everyday lives transformed, so that the world can see that transformation. You are not 'just' a woman with hardships, sorrows, rejections, and disappointments. Whatever your struggles may be, you are a woman of God. He has created every woman since the foundation of this world. These stories have trials and testing - and you will be encouraged to move forward with God's help.

The title, 'I'm Waiting for You,' is exactly that! Do all the women in the book find a husband? If not, we should not be discouraged because God has another amazing journey for them and, for us!

I hope you enjoy reading this book as much as I have enjoyed writing it.

'God is love.'
1 John 4:8 (NIV)

ACKNOWLEDGEMENT

Special people helped with editing these stories: Simone Gracie, Mirta Gladding, Karen Curran, Rob Davidson, Juliana Gualda, James Leffler, Rob Martin and Gemma Curran.

I value your time and friendship.

Many thanks for sharing your expertise with me.

ABOUT THE AUTHOR

Adela M Robinson is passionate about Jesus and about writing. She has always wanted to write a book to minister God's truth, hope and healing to women.

Adela has a huge heart for women and children. She longs to see women move from dreaming with God into dedicated action. In recent years she has birthed, laboured and brought about women's conferences in both the UK and America. She has prepared for these with prayer, detail and deep thoughtfulness. Her desire is for women to know that they are profoundly and intensely loved by God.

In 'I'm Waiting For You,' her first work of fiction, Adela deals with the often-overlooked issues that single Christian women face, especially those longing for a husband. Interwoven into the stories is God's love for each woman as he brings people into their lives to minister to them in their hurt and brokenness.

Adela and I have been prayer partners for many years, praying weekly both in person and across continents. As her prayer partner, I join with her prayer for this book: as you read it, whether or not you know Jesus, may you know God's peace beyond all understanding; may you know that you are passionately loved and receive hope and healing; and may God provide for you and fulfil you in incredible, unexpected and joyful ways.

Karen Mary Hudson

REBECCA
The Kiss

"Many waters cannot quench love; rivers cannot sweep it away."
(Song of Solomon 8:7 NIV)

My heart skipped a beat the first time I met Carl. I couldn't stop looking at him. We were at a friend's costume party. He was dressed as James Bond, with dark glasses, and I was dressed as Cinderella in an old torn long dress. Intense feelings of attraction had struck me when my eyes sank into his deep gaze.

Loud music boomed as people mingled and chattered at the Windwhistle Inn, in Chard, Somerset. Some people were already on the dance floor bopping to the beats.

It wasn't long after I arrived that Carl made his way towards me, holding a pint of beer as he weaved his way cunningly through the crowd. My first words to him were, 'You're the prince,' I laughed, 'And I must be the pauper!' We both burst into laughter.

Yes, I did eventually fall deeply in love with this strong, irresistible man.

On our first date, I wore a brightly coloured, short-sleeved, knee-length dress paired with black leather high heels and my favourite jewellery and purse. Carl complimented me at every opportunity.

'Wow you look incredible,' he would dote, 'I love how you've done your nails!'

He was a mature twenty-seven-year-old and I was a youthful twenty-two. He appreciated my easy-going nature, great sense of humour and my ability to get on with anyone I met.

Carl was an expert at making me laugh. I hadn't stopped laughing that entire evening. His admiring eyes never left my glowing face. By the end of the night my jaw ached, but what a beautiful ache it was.

His respect for me boosted my confidence beyond my imagination. His values were aligned with mine – his loyalty to his family and his love for people.

Being a jovial man, Carl was ideal for me. Sometimes I tightly closed my eyes and opened them again to see whether I had been dreaming… not daring to believe a man could really make me feel so happy.

We had so much in common – like the fact we were both church goers. His parents had been missionaries in Brazil, where Carl had spent most of his childhood. (I loved the way he spoke in Portuguese, I had no idea what he was saying, but his eyes said it all.) I had grown up with committed Christian parents and two siblings in rural Somerset.

After six stupendous months dating, Carl broached the subject of marriage.

'Have you ever thought of getting married?'

'Yes...' my sparkling eyes told him.

I was convinced I would marry him. I felt secure and relaxed in his company and trusted him completely. He had made me feel valued, important, respected, worthy and loved, especially on days when I had low self-esteem. Every time I saw him my heart fluttered. *How many people can make you feel extraordinary?* Only Carl could do that for me, no one else. I would do anything for him - all he had to do was to ask. I was completely enamoured.

One day, Carl surprised me at my parents' home. I was lying on a comfy deck chair in their walled garden when he arrived and went down on one knee. Reaching into the pocket of his white summer jacket, he produced a small, red box. Opening it, he charmingly asked, 'Will you marry me?' I stole a glance at the shiny gold band with clusters of crystals – pure, enchanting diamonds. Capturing the sunlight, the engagement ring sparkled at me and my smile beamed back; the ring fitted perfectly on my finger.

We soon started planning our idyllic wedding ceremony. I hadn't known I could experience such deep affection and love for a man.

+ + +

Shopping for my wedding dress with my mum and older sister was one of the best times of my life. It made the prospect of marriage more real.

My spectacular ivory wedding gown hung in the closet. It had mesmerized me by its beauty. The exquisite strapless dress had back lacing, an embroidered bodice, a breathtakingly beautiful, ruffled skirt with layers of netting to provide fullness and an exquisite train. I used to take it out of the garment bag now and again to admire and delight in it, smiling and dreaming excitedly of our romantic wedding day.

A few days after the dress shopping, we had decided to celebrate our relationship of ten months and ten days. Double ten was all the excuse we needed to pop the cork on a bottle of champagne! It felt like the perfect way to finish our romantic meal at a high-class Brazilian restaurant.

'Looks like I'll be inheriting a new mum and dad,' said Carl, reaching for the bottle. I polished off my drink and he generously refilled my glass.

'A great mum and dad at that!' he grinned.

'Mind you Carl, your parents aren't too bad either!!'

We had a great time, and I had had a bit too much bubbly.

Carl drove us back to my place. My housemate Lisa had gone away that weekend. Previously, I had never been alone in the house with Carl. This time I was. In my heart I knew what would happen and was too tipsy, too infatuated, to care.

His lips were warm and inviting. They tasted of champagne and I was entranced. The kiss soon led us to the bedroom. I wanted to please him. Sure, it was great. After all, we were engaged to be married and it felt right in the moment.

From then on it felt only natural to sleep together regularly. He praised me in the bedroom. How empowering it was for me to hear those words! How easy it had been for me to give myself to him!

However, sometimes, our actions lead to unforeseen consequences. This certainly was the case for me, and it all started with a drink and a kiss. At that moment nothing could have prepared me for how things were going to change.

After nine delightful months of wedding planning, and with only one month to go, Carl said he wanted to have a serious talk with me. Nothing could have prepared my heart for what he had to say. We arranged to meet at my home that evening, around 6.30pm.

He couldn't get the edge out of his voice, 'It's over. I don't love you anymore.'

'Wh...at! What do you mean, it's... it's over?' My eyes filled with intensity. *Was this a bad dream?!* I fought to compose myself. I shuddered as if someone had poured cold water down the nape of my back. *How could he stab me in the heart like this? Did I do something wrong?*

I walked towards him, shaking inside. I pretended I didn't hear what he had said and tentatively reached my arms to encircle his neck. My throat closed tight. He was like a mannequin. I glared into his troubled eyes.

'I love you more than anything in the world and want you in my life.' My voice quavered at every word.

He reached determinedly for my hands and flung them heavily to my side. *How could he hurt me? Was this the same Carl I fell in love with?* He walked away slowly and stood beside the leather settee. His steely eyes pierced my very soul as my pleading looks begged answers in reply.

Confused, my nervous lips asked him, 'What have I done? I don't understand?' He didn't respond. I had given my all to him, my soul and my body. I was completely destroyed, devastated. I wished the ground would open and swallow me. My boat of blissful joy was rocked, capsized, and shipwrecked on the bitter rocks of rejection. *How could this be?*

My frustrated tears turned swiftly to anger.

I shouted loudly, 'Say something!'

No reply. Carl silently tightened his lips and narrowed his eyes. He sulked on, standing imposingly to his full height, arms crossed defensively under a lifted chest.

Somehow, I managed to lift my paralysed feet as I hauled them heavily around the room asking questions.

'Is there someone else? Had you known all along you weren't going to marry me? … Did you… did you? Answer me,' I shrieked, 'say something!!' All kinds of questions raced out increasing the volume of my voice, and Carl stood wordlessly like a robot. I was so agitated with him. Head bent, his eyes darted to and fro, never brave enough to look me straight in the face.

From the mantlepiece, the clock I inherited from my grandfather chimed 7.00pm. Oh how differently Carl was treating me than my lovely old grandfather did.

Carl walked briskly towards me. I came up to his chest, as he at last found the courage to stare into my eyes. He tucked the strand of hair behind my ear and framed my face with his hands, leaned down and kissed me hard. Mixed emotions overwhelmed me. *What does this mean?* His gaze penetrated through me, accelerating the pounding of my heart. A muscle jerked in his jaw as he smiled bleakly.

A tear had surfaced in his eye. 'I'm sorry…' and turned towards the door, his voice broken, yet final, as he said, 'Goodbye.' I jolted as the door slammed, rocking the picture of the two of us on our weekend away, until it fell to the ground and smashed. The finality of the broken glass and his brazen words pierced me like a two-edged sword and slashed my heart in two.

A kiss is reserved only for those in your deepest affections. Why kiss me if he had no intention of caring for me? The kiss was a betrayal. *Why did he have to leave me with that memory?*

My eyes were on fire. My shoulders hunched. I sank into the sofa shivering as if I had come out of a freezing shower. It was like a dream – a nightmare! – wondering what had happened. *Had he met someone else? Did I do something wrong to change his feelings towards me? Did he just use me?*

Carl had been my security, each lovely word, gesture or touch was like a brick in the wall that protected me. My walls suddenly crumbled down one brick at a time, before my eyes, until I was exposed. My confidence in who I was slipped away as an inner, vulnerable me was left exposed to the elements.

Now I had to protect myself. I never want to feel this devastation again – no words could describe how I felt. *Why had he done this to me? Why? Why?*

Deep down inside I had always been insecure and self-conscious about my weight. I had done everything to please Carl... Now I had lost him, but it felt like I'd lost myself too.

In my eyes, the sky was no longer blue, but sickly green; the grass was no longer green but ghostly blue. My life had been turned upside down in a snap.

+ + +

After our relationship ended, I found out that Carl had cancelled the reception hall and outside caterers, he even cancelled the honeymoon. It was all too much for me and every day I was teary and low.

Colleagues from work, who were invited to the wedding, contacted me, 'hey, how are you doing…'

They didn't really know how to start the conversation.

'Fine,' I replied. I didn't want to engage in a conversation. How I survived I don't know. My flatmate Lisa was supportive and noticed I was putting on weight.

'You've been at those biscuits again.'

I smiled weakly, 'Only a few!' I never thought anything of it. I pondered later over what she had said and realised I had missed a period and had put it down to stress.

For peace of mind, I went to the chemist and bought a pregnancy test. I discovered a devastating blow, I was pregnant. The test must be wrong so I did another one. Positive. I sat on the bathtub. The shock of this news had wrenched my heart. *How could I have this baby? How could I not have this baby... his baby... our baby!* There was a fight of wills between right and wrong inside me.

Being in agony over what to do was like being in a fierce contest with two wrestlers in a ring. I had been putting up a fight. I couldn't depend on Carl to help me decide, *or could I?* He was the father. *How could I have been so blind not to have seen that our relationship was coming to an end? What was I to do - keep the baby or terminate the pregnancy?*

Carl had told me he didn't love me. Yet I missed him so much. The pain was unbearable. My love for him hadn't diminished but grew stronger. *How could that be possible after what he had done to me? Would anything change now I was pregnant?*

A few weeks later, I found the strength and met up with Carl. He asked me to meet him in the cinema lobby, of all places!

'I'm pregnant.' I said nothing else.

He fidgeted and growled, 'So this is your way of hooking me back into a relationship I don't want with you!'

'That's not true. I'm pregnant.' I could hardly believe my ears but what else was I to expect. 'I'm telling you the truth.'

'I don't want the baby,' And he sharply bellowed, 'Get rid of it!'

The blood rushed to my crumpling face. I could feel the pitying, judging stares of passers-by. I felt exposed all over again. Carl hastily walked away with his hands concealed in his trouser pockets.

Later that night, I turned restlessly in bed agonising over what to do. My world had been ripped apart, like a weathered rope torn ruthlessly into fraying fragments, it's former strength and beauty rotten away. I didn't know what to do or where to turn. God seemed far away. He must have rejected me too. He didn't care for me, just like Carl. Eventually, I fell into an uneasy sleep with a heavy heart and unsettled dreams.

In my heart I wanted to tell my mother, but I was too ashamed. People in my church gossiped about girls getting pregnant out of marriage. I was one of them! *What would they say if they found out that a Christian girl from a respectable Christian home was pregnant? Would Carl deny he was the father?* Carl didn't want me or the baby. Rejected by my lover, and now I felt rejected by the church too.

Eventually, the struggle was over. I tossed and turned over and over in my mind what was the best option. I couldn't bear this torment any longer. I had decided. I felt I had no other choice. I made an appointment for an abortion.

It was a cloudy Tuesday afternoon when I went to the clinic. The day the dustbin men came with their screeching lorry. I had taken a few days off work as leave.

On the way there in the car, I had passed my local church without a second glance, wondering... *if they only knew, what would they think?* Shoppers laden with bags hurried here and there, and everyone looked cheerful – except me! Despite all the people around me I felt abandoned. I toughened myself and numbed my emotions.

Before the abortion appointment, two weeks ago, I had previously met with a nurse and doctor. We spoke about whether abortion was a right decision for me, and what my abortion options would be.

They had examined me and I had an ultrasound to find out how far into the pregnancy I had gone. Seven weeks.

Now here I was, sat in the waiting room unaccompanied but surrounded by other girls with their supporting friends and family members.

When I finally entered the room to have the termination, the doctor asked me why I was alone. I bowed my head in shame, and sunk my voice to a whisper. I told her that I was too afraid to speak to my family, and therefore wanted to do it alone. A nurse in the room was kind and supportive – she held my hand throughout the procedure. I was so thankful she was there for me.

+ + +

After the abortion, I was worn out with the stress of the day. I woke up in the middle of the night thinking I heard a baby crying... it was the neighbour's new puppy whimpering. Staring sightlessly into the darkness, I crawled wearily back under the covers, curling into a protective ball. I squeezed my eyes closed, and cried myself back to sleep.

A great heavy blanket engulfed my whole being, covering my secret. No one knew except me, Carl and God. The guilt and condemnation were overwhelming. The grief of losing my baby was unexpected, yet it had been my choice... I had no choice? I cannot turn the clock back. But... but... I had no choice, right?

No one knew I had been intimate with Carl. We both claimed to be Christians and I couldn't face the shame and stares. If I had known how all this would have ended, I would never had slept with Carl. No one told me it would be a torturous heartache, having to live with this ever-gnawing guilt.

Carl this is your fault! What have you done to us? I secretly blamed Carl for all this. I couldn't face him again, so I buried the pain and the blame and the rage. I so wanted to talk it over with someone, but I couldn't trust anyone. I felt too humiliated to tell my mum. I couldn't speak to family or close friends. *They would judge me, wouldn't they?* I tried to talk to God, but He abandoned me to empty silence. I felt so condemned. I am so alone.

WHAT DID REBECCA DO?

Rebecca had been betrayed. She felt forced by shame and isolation to have an abortion. The experience was emotionally painful, and she buried it all. She felt it was easier to keep a secret than to talk to anyone. She bottled up the shame and humiliation and carried it with her.

Romans 8:38-39 (TLB) says, "...Our fears for today, our worries about tomorrow, or where we are—high above the sky, or in the deepest ocean—nothing will ever be able to separate us from the love of God demonstrated by our Lord Jesus Christ when he died for us."

Matthew 7:7-9 (GNT) says, "Ask, and you will receive; seek, and you will find; knock, and the door will be opened to you. For everyone who asks will receive, and anyone who seeks will find, and the door will be opened to those who knock. Would any of you who are fathers give your son a stone when he asks for bread?"

Rebecca also had low self-esteem; she had no confidence in her self-worth. She took her identity and security from a man rather than from the creator, God. She failed to see that, whatever situation she was in, God was with her and he would be her confidence.

Joshua 1:9 (NIV) says, "Be strong and courageous. Do not be afraid; do not be discouraged, for the LORD your God will be with you wherever you go."

Psalm 139:7-8 (GNT) says, "Where could I go to escape from you? Where could I get away from your presence? If I went up to heaven, you would be there; if I lay down in the world of the dead, you would be there."

Psalm 86:1 (GNT) says, "Listen to me Lord and answer me, for I am helpless and weak."

REFLECTION

> Do you identify with Rebecca?
> Can you think of a time when you were faced with a decision that made you feel like you were caught between a rock and a hard place?
> Was God or a close friend there with you in the situation or did you struggle to make a decision alone?

Maybe you feel guilty because of a set of circumstances you found yourself in, whether it be sex before marriage, adultery or abortion.

"Be merciful to me, O God, because of your constant love…" (Psalm 51:1 GNT). (This psalm talks about King David facing the same feeling of guilt because of what he had done.)

God doesn't condemn you. His love for you won't change because of something you did. "Therefore, there is now no condemnation for those who are in Christ Jesus" (Romans 8:1 NIV).

WORDS OF WISDOM

Ask God to help you make the right decisions and ask for boldness in decision-making. Ask God to give you the strength and the will-power to trust He is working to help you in your decisions.

Ask God to show you how precious you are to Him. He accepts you just the way you are.

"May the God of hope fill you with all joy and peace as you trust in him, so that you may overflow with hope by the power of the Holy Spirit" (Romans 15:13 NIV).

Prayer: God, I need your help. I have made mistakes in my life, and I ask you to forgive me. Help me to forgive others who have hurt me too. Please cleanse me and make me whole again. In Jesus' name. Amen.

A WOMAN NOT CONDEMNED

John 8:2-11 (NIV)

"At dawn he appeared again in the temple courts, where all the people gathered round him, and he sat down to teach them. The teachers of the law and the Pharisees brought in a woman caught in adultery. They made her stand before the group and said to Jesus, 'Teacher, this woman was caught in the act of adultery. In the Law Moses commanded us to stone such women. Now what do you say?' They were using this question as a trap, in order to have a basis for accusing him.

But Jesus bent down and started to write on the ground with his finger. When they kept on questioning him, he straightened up and said to them, 'Let any one of you who is without sin be the first to throw a stone at her.' Again, he stooped down and wrote on the ground.

At this, those who heard began to go away one at a time, the older ones first, until only Jesus was left, with the woman still standing there. Jesus straightened up and asked her, 'Woman, where are they? Has no one condemned you?'

'No one, sir,' she said.

'Then neither do I condemn you,' Jesus declared. 'Go now and leave your life of sin.'"

"I, even I, am He who blots out your transgressions for My own sake; And I will not remember your sins."
(Isaiah 43:25 NKJV)[1]

---

[1] You may wish to access Christian counselling services to help you work through past decisions and grow in confidence. Here are some suggested organisations. Christian Counsellors UK: www.wellhealing.org, www.lighthousechristiancare.co.uk, www.waverleyabbeycollege.ac.uk/find-a-counsellor. Christian Counsellors USA: www.focusonthefamily.com/counseling-services-and-referrals

JULIA
A Second Chance

"I will be your God throughout your lifetime – until your hair is white with age. I made you, and I will care for you. I will carry you along and save you."
(Isaiah 46:4 NLT)

My charges, Oscar and Bella, were bubbly children and laughed breathlessly when they enjoyed outdoor activities. Their parents were loving and kind, traits amply reflected in their children. Being their nanny, I accompanied Oscar and Bella everywhere possible to educate them. I was thrilled to be loved by them as much as I too loved them. I cherished life with them.

Yet, as I watched the stars dazzle at night, lighting up the night sky, and the moon's soothing splendour, I realised I was God's ultimate workmanship, His treasure, to be admired and adored. He made me and cared for me.

There was so much in the world for me to explore, and I craved to experience everything for myself. I yearned to travel, make new acquaintances, and come alive! I knew in my heart that it may not be all that I imagined it to be, but I was restless and fascinated.

What would my absence mean for Bella and Oscar, especially since I had been with them from birth? Would it be a profound shock for them? I was torn, as I loved my job.

However, I knew I would always wonder what I was missing and desperately wanted to find out for myself.

After months of struggling with my desires and choices, I made up my mind. I knew Oscar and Bella would miss me, but surely, I had to think of myself and what was best for me? And, after all, I could easily be replaced.

The day of departure finally arrived. As a Christian, I wasn't sure whether I was doing the right thing. I hadn't prayed for guidance from God or asked any responsible adult in the church I attended if I was making the right choice. I tried to ignore that inner voice telling me not to venture into this journey. The temptation, however, thrilled me, and the tug on my heart was unyielding.

To fulfil my dream, I had made up my mind and was changing residence to move to the new and exciting world of London, which I hungered to explore, ignoring my nudging suspicion and the scripture I learnt as a child, "Do not love the world or anything in the world. If anyone loves the world, the love of the Father is not in them. For everything in the world – the lust of the flesh, the lust of the eyes and the pride of life – comes not from the Father but from the world. The world and its desires pass away, but whoever does the will of God lives forever."

It was then I planned my future. The world was more appealing than God. I wanted to live.

But leaving was worse than I had expected. The children were distraught. They understood why I was leaving, but the reality hit them hard. It tore my heart too. I was nervous to be travelling into the world all by myself, as I had always been with someone, yet I was joyful about the new prospects ahead.

+ + +

And just like that, a year passed in a flash. I still enjoyed touring the big city with its charming buildings, attractive entertainment venues and delectable restaurants. I adored strolling in Hyde Park, as it reminded me of innocent Oscar and Bella.

Socialising in the city, I made many friends by joining tourist attraction trips, along with aerobics and painting classes. Soon, I developed a smoking habit. Friendships and acceptance were very important to me, and smoking was a gateway to social inclusion when we went out partying together and visited nightclubs.

When we started smoking I suspected it wasn't good. At first, it felt wonderful to have experienced such euphoria, but it didn't last long and, ultimately, made me gloomy. I eventually started craving more, despite hallucinating at times.

It had all started on a game night at someone's home. I had tagged along with my friends and had been persuaded to try my first joint. I didn't understand exactly what it was, but I trusted my friends – big mistake! As I smoked it, I began to choke slightly but continued to act the part without realising that my lust for it was growing.

It was approaching midnight, and the house was still crowded. I sat on the sofa slumped over like a dizzy cat spun around a thousand times. Relaxed yet exhilarated, I started giggling to myself in a childlike way. All the while, I ignored any promptings that I felt were from God.

The truth was my friends wanted to escape from reality, their unhappiness, and for them, gratifying the lust of their flesh was the answer. I also wanted to forget my loneliness. Even though I had friends, my heart ached. I didn't realise that kicking this overpowering habit of dope would be more difficult than I expected.

Soon, I grew accustomed to the drugs and had a nearly fatal accident. I had been delirious on my way home from the library. Giddy and high as a kite, I had felt invincible and strolled to the town's local bridge in an inebriated state. I grabbed onto the top of the railings with both hands and climbed up the lower railings. I manoeuvred myself and rested my rear on the upper rail, waving my arms in the air, swaying in the wind like a broken tree.

Loud voices rose around me, like blaring music in a rock concert, drowning my peace. I gasped as suddenly a pair of muscular arms gripped me tightly around my waist. We both plummeted on our sides on the hard concrete. Even though I was hurting from the impact of the fall, I giggled. I don't remember what I said exactly, but I guess they weren't pleasant words. Somehow, the man managed to restrain me as I fought to break free of this rude awakening.

The police were called. I ended up at a police station in a cell, as they couldn't make any sense of my jabbering. The next morning, I realised this hallucination was a reality. My side ached as I lay on a lumpy bed.

Remembering the events of last night, I woke up alarmed, and jerked upright at my surroundings. Head hammering like a drum, I wiped haphazardly at my eyes with the back of my hand fighting to see where I was. A police cell.

Grubby walls engulfed me. Peeling paint ripped down the walls. In my frustration I yearned to yank down the rest. Black mould beaded the ceiling like a soiled polka dot dress. The potent smell of stale air mixed with a tinge of cheap perfume made me nauseated. I coughed quietly.

A young lady sat staring at me as I faced towards her cell. Two empty cells were on either side of her. Her dirty blond hair showed her dark roots. She wore a colourful print dress covering her print leggings; a vintage cardi covered her arms. Her all-seeing gaze was hidden behind her classy glasses. I wondered what she had done to be in here.

'You alright?'

I was startled at the volume of her stammering voice. She turned my way as if searching my eyes. She sat perched on the end of the bed.

I hesitated to say anything at first and clung to the bedding.

'Yes, I think so,' I responded.

'I'm Sarah. What you in here for?' as her hands grasped the edge of the bedframe as she swung her dangling feet.

I stumbled out, 'I'm Julia. I'm…I'm in here for public disorder, the cops would probably say.'

'I'm in for drunk and disorder. This aint my first time. The bluebottles are used to me.'

'Bluebottles?!' I queried.

'Where've you been… the cops!'

'Oh…' My cheeks burnt red… 'It's… it's my first time inside a police cell,' I shamefully admitted.

'Oh yeah!' she said as if not convinced.

'I don't intend on coming back here again, it's petrifying being behind bars.'

Although Sarah was unkempt, she was sober.

'How many times have you been in here?' I asked.

'I've lost count.' As she continued to swing her lanky legs inspecting her polished nails.

I swung my legs slowly to the hard ground, resting my arms on the bed, 'Doesn't it scare you?'

Still inspecting her nails, 'First time I got banged up… yeah I was frit, but now I aint, I've gotten used to it.'

'Have you got family?'

Sarah shuffled on the bed as she tilted her head to one corner, 'No one cares for me.'

I don't know what came over me but I said, 'God cares and loves you.'

Pouting her lips she chortled, staring me hard in the face, 'Sure He does, that's why I'm banged up in ere!'

At that moment a police officer opened the door leading to the cell area and strolled towards my cell fumbling with keys.

'You don't know how lucky you were yesterday,' growled the police officer, unlocking my cell door. He escorted me out of the cell.

'Pray for me Julia,' Sarah stammered out in a weak voice.

I turned and a smile dawned on my lips as I continued to scramble swiftly behind the officer into the main station. Once there I completed forms.

Besides a stern warning, a phone number was given to me to seek support. Never had I been inside a police cell, and never before had I been so petrified of what drugs could do to the mind.

My beauty had begun to fade. My once sparkling eyes were now dull and unexciting. This was the detrimental effects of taking drugs. *How was I to escape this path of life?*

+ + +

My friends regularly gravitated to the pub like magnets. Although I wasn't a drinker, I did try a glass of whiskey. It was surprisingly strong, and I coughed like crazy, holding my slim hand against my chest gulping in air. My cheeks flushed as my friends pointed and laughed at me. Squinting, I held the glass to my mouth and hesitantly sipped until the glass was empty.

I wanted them to love and accept me. I wanted to be part of their society. Deep down, I wasn't happy and neither were my friends. We were all looking for an escape route and, in a sense, found ourselves together. A thin veneer of fun did little to disguise our desperation.

They teased me when they learnt that at twenty-four, though I had had boyfriends, I had never slept with any of them. They laughed at me mercilessly. The blood ran to my cheeks like someone lighting a furnace. I tried hard not to shed a single tear, excused myself and dashed to the ladies' bathroom.

I stood in front of the mirror and stared at myself. A tear rolled down my face. I hastily brushed it away. My handbag contained my 'special' cigarettes. I took one out. My hand trembled as I lit it. It helped me escape and forget my humiliation. When I came to my senses, I was confident enough to face my friends again. *Was this what being accepted in society was about? Is this how the rest of the world lived?*

No one had even noticed my sadness, as they were too busy with their own lives to find the time to see mine. If God had been in my life, I would have been intact. He would have cared for me.

When I returned to the bar, I didn't even realise that someone had spiked my drink. Some of my friends said their goodbyes and started leaving the pub. I couldn't focus. Woozy, I ambled to a cushioned chair at a table and flopped down. Someone in the pub strolled towards me and asked lazily if they could take me home. I stumbled over my words and said, 'No... thanks.' I didn't know the stranger towering over me.

Intoxicated, I somehow staggered back to the ladies' bathroom and checked my face in the mirror. My eyes popped out with fright. For an instant, I couldn't even recognise myself. In a daze, I pushed open the cubicle door and, with unsteady movements, managed to sit on the uncomfortable toilet seat until I could regain some sense. Drums banged furiously in my head.

Sometime later, I heard loud noises of furniture being moved, so I forced myself off the seat and went to investigate. The pub was closing for the night. Everyone had left. It must have been late. I could hear the rain pounding on the rooftop and windowpanes, straining to get in. *How was I going to get home?*

I swayed towards the door wearily, and pushed it open with great effort as it bounced back heavily against my arm. The pain was excruciating. *Was my arm broken?*

I stepped outside in the heavy rain with no covering, only my flimsy summer dress. I paused outside, disorientated in the dull darkness. The girl who had dropped us off at the pub in her sports car was nowhere to be found. She had probably thought I would be able to get home by myself or that I had left when, in actuality, I had been hung up in the bathroom. Moreover, where was I?

Trepidation filled me from head to toe. My heart thumped so loudly I could hear the rhythm of the beat in my ears. Logically, I had to stay focused, but my imagination was running wild. In the cold torrential rain pouring over me like a ship being sunk at sea, I knew I needed God. Tears streamed down my sad face.

I had been happiest in the presence of God, which was heaven to me. He created me and loved me. I had always been cared for, and accepted for who I was. No one adored me as He did. I wanted to be cherished, valued and special to someone, and all this I had with God. *Would He listen to me?* I longed for Him in my hour of need.

Bewildered, I wandered the dim streets aimlessly. I tried hard not to cry and blur my vision. I needed to see which direction to walk in. Why did God give me emotions? I dared not have my special cigarette to forget this dreadful moment; it could snuff out my life completely.

The stinging storm was ferocious, like an angry bear bearing down on me. My beautiful hair was soaked and lifeless. Water rushed over my head and drenched me from head to toe. My kitten heel shoes were squishy and my aching feet cold. Which direction was I to take next? North, south? Nothing looked familiar. Which way was I to turn? Holding my painful arm, I continued to push my body. I needed to shelter myself from the storm.

My strength and energy were gradually ebbing away. I approached an elegantly dressed young couple, hoping they would rescue me, but they swiftly crossed the road. A car sped by, drenching me further by splashing grimy water from a huge puddle lying vacant on the road. A few minutes later, I hailed a taxi, but it passed me by as if I didn't exist.

Alone and afraid, the storm hammered down on me as if to make me fade away. Earnestly, I longed for God and called out faintly to Him in prayer. My whisper sounded loud in my empty heart.

Why had I not seen I had been complete with God before? How could I have forgotten Him so quickly? I missed His presence and my special times of talking with Him. I was always happy with Him.

Somehow, I discovered shelter in the doorway of a derelict building. The other tall buildings surrounding me were splattered with graffiti. I quickly surveyed the several empty spaces where windows would have stood. Soaked newspapers littered the street. A shoe, turned on its side, lay in the thundering rain. Something scurried by – was it a rat or a cat, or just my imagination?

I sat huddled in a corner, out of sight, stumbling in and out of consciousness. The cold wind rushed against my face. I needed to gain control, raise myself and start walking again, but my sore arm hurt badly. I nearly fainted with the pain. *When would this relentless storm stop? Was the storm a reflection of my life?*

I knew I must not sleep, yet my body screamed to lie down and slumber. But I had to keep myself awake. I tried my hardest to stand. Unsuccessful, I crumpled in a painful heap on the dirty slippery floor. Excruciating pain pulsated through my arm.

The patter of the silver raindrops was melodic music to my ears. Tears tumbled down my cheeks and kept in time with the slow and steady rhythm of the raindrops. I was weary of this life and could not move. I had to lie down, for a brief moment, and rest my spiritless body. I struggled to suppress the urge to close my eyes… my eyelids fluttered and then closed to the sound of the rain.

+ + +

After an unknown amount of time, I turned my head and slowly pried open my eyes, blinking the darkness away. I adjusted my eyes and glanced at the person touching my hand. My eyes widened. I didn't know the woman who was smiling at me.

'Where am I?'

'You're in a hospital.'

I observed this stranger with a kind face, still holding my hand, then stared at the cast on my other arm and asked, 'Who are you?'

'My name is Ann, and I am a street pastor.'

'A what?' I exclaimed faintly.

She smiled gently as she said, 'A street pastor looks after people in the community. They are trained volunteers from local churches, who care about their community. We basically go out into the community, no matter the weather, taking supplies with us, to help those out on the streets and listen to them. Something prompted my colleagues and I to go to the derelict building on our patrol, and there we found you.'

'I'm glad you did, thank you.'

'You were in a serious condition, and they didn't know whether you would live or die. I stayed with you and prayed that God would spare your life.'

'God heard my cry!' I exclaimed.

'What do you mean?' Ann responded.

'I called out to God in my despair, and He heard me because He sent you.'

Ann smiled broadly, 'I too would like to think He did. The doctors said you are going to be OK.'

All I could say was thank you God, for hearing and answering my cry, and for giving me another chance. Looks like God was watching over me all the time, waiting for me to call on Him.

Sarah quickly came to my mind. I knew there and then that my relationship with God would be restored. He heard my cry and rescued me; I knew He would hear my cry for Sarah and one day will rescue her and transform her life.

Tears of joy streamed down my happy face faster than stallions running free in an open field. I didn't have to hide them from Him. He knew everything about me and still accepted me. I had been lost, but my Maker had found me.

All this time, I had had everything with my Maker that I could ever imagine or desire, yet I hadn't known.

God mended my brokenness and healed my wounds. I would never leave Him. He would never leave me nor forsake me. I gave God praise for all He had done for me.

REFLECTION

> Do you identify in any way with Julia?
> Have you been in a similar situation where you ran away to get more out of life, only to find that it wasn't what you expected?
> Do you feel unaccepted by others around you?

Julia was a Christian, and she worked as a nanny. However, she believed that there was more to life than the life she was living. She had never experienced what it was to live in "the world" and thought she was missing out on all the joys it had to offer.

Julia's life had started off well, but when she ventured deeper into the world, she realised it wasn't what she had hoped to find. She had left God behind and experimented with alcohol and drugs to be part of society and accepted by others. She then understood that this wasn't the life she had dreamt of. This life was vacuous and lonely. The young ladies in the story had lost their way in the world and were trying to find fulfilment in it.

Unhappy, Julia could not find what she was looking for. The more she experimented with drugs, the more her life kept oozing away from her and the more broken her body became. The life she had had with God, she realised, was the life she should be living, the life that gave her joy, peace, fulfilment and purpose. The life she thought would be better was a life ending in misery.

Although Julia was lost and in despair, she cried out to God and He came and found her.

PRODIGAL DAUGHTER

Luke 15:11-24

"I was lost but Jesus found me."
(cf. Luke 10:19)

Most of us have heard the story of the prodigal son. It could easily have been a prodigal daughter! A father had two daughters and his younger daughter wanted her portion of her inheritance from her father. The father gave the portion to his daughter. The daughter left home, and she spent the money on wild living. She thought the grass was greener on the other side. She soon ran out of money and had to take a job looking after pigs. She realised she had sinned against heaven and her father.

She decided to go home and humble herself by working as a servant for her father. Her father had always been looking for her return, and when he saw his daughter coming home in the distance, he was full of love and compassion. He ran to meet her. He was extremely overjoyed to see his daughter and hugged and kissed her. He didn't even give his daughter time to fully explain why she had returned, but he heard his daughter's words of repentance. The real issue wasn't the money she had wasted but the relationship she had broken. The father restored his daughter to her rightful place and her daughtership.

WORDS OF WISDOM

The father never reminded his daughter of her past – he just loved her. Our heavenly Father, God, doesn't remind us of our past, He just continues to love us.

I can almost hear the Father say to His once lost daughter, 'I am honoured to be your Father and I am honoured to have you as my child.'

Prayer: Lord, thank you for loving me in such a way that I can never fully understand. Let your love sink deep into my soul, my inner being so that it overwhelms me and draws me closer to you. In Jesus' name. Amen.

COLLETTE
The Watch

"For God so loved the world that he gave his one and only Son, that whoever believes in him shall not perish but have eternal life."
(John 3:16 NIV)

After a hearty lunch, I lounged snugly in an old, stained mahogany rocking chair, casting a silhouette on the window behind. Squishy cushions cuddled behind my tired back and sides, as I lulled into a satisfying and peaceful sleep. The room was still and quiet but for the faint chatter of next door's TV. On my lap rested a worn covered book – a crime novel.

Sometime later I began to stir softly, like a cat waking from a gratifying nap, in the dimly lit L-shaped lounge at my Nan's home.

The faint light, from the oval window behind me, reflected on the polished wooden floor.

The sparse room had modest furniture: a television, a three-seater mauve sofa, two small matching coffee tables and a colourful vintage rug that Nan was given as a wedding present from her parents over fifty-years ago. To the left of me was the magnolia-painted wall where Nan had artfully displayed pictures of the family including Emily, my only child, who was in the centre of all the pictures.

The dining room to the right faced the garden. Emily's Great Nanna Annie – still mostly just 'Nan' to me! - liked to sit in the dining room admiring her well-kept garden, one of her many hobbies.

Relaxed, I stretched out my skinny arms, yawning like a toddler, safe and secure. I rubbed my tired eyes, slowly blinking to focus clearly. At lunch it had been warm enough to open a window, and I suppose Nan hadn't closed it since the chilly autumn air cut through the room.

Nan's half knitted jumper sprawled on the sofa, an unwitting caricature of me unravelled on the rocking chair.

I heard her humming sweetly in the country kitchen as the whiff of freshly baked cakes wafted out through the open door. Nan loved to bake her own recipes and was generous in sharing her bakes amongst the community. The elderly neighbours eagerly anticipated a variety of newly baked, mouth-watering cakes each week.

The hours had passed whilst I slept and it was almost 4.00pm, the time I was meeting Samantha for our photography class at Devon Photography School. Samantha and I had lived in the same street as children, and we remained good friends.

My thick sleeved jumper had kept my legs warm while I napped. I pulled it over my head and stretched my arms into the sleeves. The collar hugged my neck cosily. I shuffled myself from the seat, dashed upstairs, changed into some clean skinny jeans, and pushed my warm feet into my cold trainers. With hands on hips, *I wonder where my camera is?* I found it buried under an old shirt I had slung on the floor.

Holding on to the railing I bolted down the stairs to the sweet aroma of Nan's cakes. As I hurried into the kitchen, Nan was busy placing her famous scones on a cooling rack.

'I'm off to my class, Nan,' I said cheerfully, planting a firm kiss on her cheek. 'Cakes look great!' Greedily, I grabbed one and stuffed it into my welcoming mouth as I wriggled into my thick jacket. Nan tapped the back of my hand gently with a wooden spoon, raising her brows with a bright smile.

'You better take another one for later on,' she said, beaming. 'Have you got your phone?'

Nan knew I could be absent-minded. 'Yes, I have.'

'Have you got your sandwiches? I made you your favourite – bacon, lettuce and tomato.'

'Yes, got that in my bag, thanks Nan, you're the best. See you later!' as I placed another grateful kiss on her cheek.

With the camera strap over my neck and a rucksack slung on my shoulder, I rushed out the front door, down the short drive and onto the street pavement. I quickened my steps toward the number twenty-three bus stop in my hometown of Exeter.

+ + +

Emily stayed with her father every two weeks, living with Nan and me the rest of the time, a mile from my parents. That once-a-fortnight break was a well-needed rest for Nan and me when we could get some time for ourselves.

I remember when I found out I was pregnant by my long-term boyfriend, Mark. I was initially shocked as it wasn't planned – but thrilled at the thought of becoming a mum. I was thirty then; my parents were so excited and overjoyed. The pressure of getting ready for a new baby strained my relationship with Mark, and sadly he wasn't ready to stick it out with us. In the end, I moved back home.

Living with my parents was stressful. We did *not* get on. Mum and I were too much alike. We had too many emotional and aggressive arguments. You would think we were in a TV soap drama; we would have certainly received good ratings! Mum and I had not gotten along even before I was pregnant, and when Emily arrived, our relationship became intolerable. I loved my parents, and I knew they loved me, but we just couldn't live together.

The constant demands of a newborn left me physically exhausted. The constant arguing made me angry and emotionally drained. Exhaustion fed the anger. The emotional strain made the night feeds that much more gruelling. I knew it wasn't positive for Emily's well-being. So, when Emily turned one, Nan suggested we move in with her, and for three years, we had been living with a sweet and understanding Great Nanna.

Nan was a devout Christian. Although I believed in some sort of God, I wasn't into the church stuff. She took Emily to a children's church on Sundays, which was fine by me, and Emily loved to attend.

Nan's face always smiled with an unexplainable lightness. There was an element of wonder in her angelic gaze, the same gaze as whenever she looked at nature. It fascinated me. *Was it to do with Jesus?* Nan talked about him enough. She bubbled with joy and lifted me up when I felt down.

Her immense generosity to me and others gave me such a warm feeling inside. She was always willing to help whoever in the community, whatever their need. Whether it was sewing, shopping for neighbours, or spending time with a lonely person.

Nan often prayed for me and Emily. One day, I popped upstairs during a TV ad break, when her bedroom door was ajar, I over-heard her as I strolled down the upstairs corridor.

'You care for them, Jesus,' she prayed, 'so may they come to know you. You know them, Lord, so I entrust them into your hands.'

My heart warmed with love for Nan when I heard her earnest words.

+ + +

I had been turning that memory over in my mind as I ambled down the street, until I realised the time and made a mad dash for the bus stop. As I arrived all hot and flustered, I noticed an agitated man looking in every direction. He strode hurriedly towards an unsuspecting elderly woman. It all happened so fast.

'Stop thief, stop!!' I hollered with horror as he ripped open the flap of the woman's bag slung across her body.

My cry startled the man, and he tugged at the bag, nearly throwing the elderly woman to the ground, but she held on to her shopping trolley as she regained her balance. He grabbed something from the bag then jerked his head towards me before scampering across the street.

A car's brakes screeched. 'Hey! Watch out mate!'

'What the hell, man,' the thief yelled, 'get out of the road,' as he jumped with frightful anger to the metallic shriek.

The younger driver's abrasive voice echoed as the man bolted down the street like a wild alley cat. Some onlookers, thank goodness, left what they were doing and chased him.

Gripping my camera with one hand and my rucksack with the other, I sprinted towards the petite woman. I tenderly touched the shoulder of her tweed coat, which had caught on something and scuffed, likely as she tumbled. She was trembling. Thankfully, she was uninjured. Other pedestrians also came by to investigate.

'Are you alright?' I asked her.

'Yeesss…' she croaked although I noticed she had gone pale with fright.

'What a… he was… those vacant eyes, oh, how frightful!,' holding both hands tightly onto the wobbly handle which must had loosened in the struggle.

'Is this a dream?'

'No,' I replied, 'it did happen.'

'Oh… oh…'

'It's ok, it's ok, he's gone now,' as I continued to rub her shoulder.

I bent down to pick up the bits and pieces that had fallen to the ground from her bag and noticed an old watch, which I picked up. 'Is this yours?'

Her eyes flashed with realisation, then relief.

'Oh, my precious watch,' she whined softly as she took the watch from me and clutched it against her bosom.

'Is there anything missing in your bag?' I asked soothingly. 'We ought to go to the police. Would you like me to accompany you to the station?'

'Oh no, I don't want to be a bother to anyone.'

She bent her head and opened her bag to see what was missing. She assured me he had taken nothing significant.

'Let me take you to the tearoom up the road for a hot drink, and perhaps we can go to the police station together,' I insisted. *I'll text Samantha later, she'll be worried where I am.*

'Oh well, yes... yes... please,' she said wearily.

'Let me help you with your trolley.'

'Oh... you don't have to do that dear,' she said grabbing the wobbly trolley handle. 'I can manage.' She rubbed her head and blinked a couple of times.

'Are you ok?' I said peering into her eyes as I stepped closer to her and touched her arm.

Her eyelids drooped, 'Yes... I'm... I'm fine, thank you dear, just slightly shaken up from all this kerfuffle.'

We arrived at the pretty little tearoom, nestled neatly on a street corner opposite the park, with a beautiful view of the autumnal trees.

Trying to comfort her, I struck up some small talk, 'My name is Collette, by the way, Collette Jukes. What a horrible thing to have happened to you today. Are you sure you're alright?'

'Ye... yes...what a frightful day! I just can't believe it... So nice to meet a kind young woman like you. I'm Joan... Joan Seaton.' She extended her hand to me as we waited to be seated.

We occupied a seat at the back where we wouldn't be disturbed. I hung my backpack on the chair and rested the camera on the spare seat next to mine as Joan and I sat down. I ordered her a strong tea and had a latte myself. She shuddered as the waiter placed the tea in front of her clasped hands.

'Oh! Oh!, yes, thank you.'

'Here,' I said as I poured the tea, 'the tea should help calm your nerves.'

Forcing a smile, she mumbled, 'Tha...Thank you, de... dear,' as she raised the cup trembling and inhaled deeply the soothing, familiar smell. She sipped and savoured the taste.

We chatted for a while about what had happened as I attempted to gather all the information. When it was noted down, I changed the subject to take her mind off the incident.

'Joan, you seem such a lovely lady. Tell me a bit more about you. Is there a lucky "Mr Joan?"'

She tucked a lock of grey hair behind her ear and rested her arms on the table. A smile curved her lips. 'Well, the watch – let me tell you! It has a story. It was given to me by an old admirer, over sixty years ago.'

Her countenance illuminated. 'We were to be married. Here, have a look,' she opened her bag and, with unsteady hands, cradled the silver watch.

She breathed a sigh, 'John was called up to serve in the war. Before he left, he gave me this watch as a reminder of our love. I was eighteen, and he was nineteen. I never heard from him again.' A tear trickled down her cheek, as sad and happy memories met and danced again in a familiar embrace.

'My parents moved from Tiverton to Exeter. We were church goers and I met John at St Peter's church in Tiverton. I didn't know where John was stationed.' Her thoughtful gaze strayed to the window. 'His letters were not forwarded to me. And there was so much to do, of course, with the war on, and not to mention Mother losing her sight. Things get away from you, don't they? In the end I was writing to him less and less frequently. I never knew if my letters got to him or not. Before I realised it, I'd stopped writing completely,' she said with regret.

'How long ago was that?'

'Oh my... nineteen forty-six, a year after the war, that's sixty-seven years ago... I don't look eighty-five do I.' We both laughed quietly.

'Did you not meet anyone else?'

'Yes, I did, but it didn't work out and he married someone else.'

'I'm sorry.'

'Don't be sorry, it didn't work out because I was still in love with John... here...' handing me the watch to take a closer look.

I glanced at her as I held the old watch. A wistful expression appeared on her face as old recollections of her lover played over in her mind. I turned over the watch and read the inscription, "To J. All my love, JP."

'JP?' I questioned.

'Yes, John Pollock. He was extremely handsome if I do say so myself.' Her eyes lit up in joy, and her mouth broke into a smile.

Our conversation captivated me. I could guess from the lines on her face she had had a hard life. Drawn into the story of these young lovers and their old love affair.

It was a delightful chat and the time got away with us. Before we knew it, it was 5.30pm and the sun was setting, so we pulled ourselves away from our cosy corner and headed for the police station. By the time we had finished at the police station it was too late for class so I called Samantha to explain my text.

'Hi Sam, you'll never believe what happened...'

+ + +

Over the next few weeks, I kept in touch with Joan by calling and visiting her – she was only a bus ride away. I came to discover she had the same light in her eyes that Nan had. *How curious.*

On my third visit to Joan's detached bungalow, I took some of Nan's cakes. We nestled around the open log fireplace, which was already kindling, finishing our hot drinks.

'Would you like to see one of John's letters?' she asked.

'Oh, yes, I'd love to!'

She rose from her green velvet armchair and collected a bundle of envelopes from the cabinet behind. They were delicately wrapped in ribbon.

'Oh, Joan!' I exclaimed. 'Your letters from John! The envelopes look so worn. So, these must have been sent to you before you moved to Exeter?'

'Yes, indeed,' she chuckled, strolling back to her seat, 'I have read them many times. Oh, I think I'm still in love with him, strange as it may sound.'

'It's not strange. It's very romantic.'

She snuggled back in her armchair, unwrapped the small bundle and surveyed each envelope.

'Look Collette, a photo of John.'

I reached forward and carefully took the photo from her. 'He is mighty handsome in his uniform.'

'Oh yes, he is, isn't he.'

'What do you think happened to John?'

'I don't really know. He had an older brother but I couldn't locate him either. In my search to try to find John I did discover that both his parents had died in the war... so sad...' she paused for a moment. 'So, it made it difficult for me to know how to trace him.'

'But you wrote many letters to him?'

'Yes I did and none were returned so I hope he received them. They had my new address on but I didn't hear anything from him... My family had changed their surname because my father had deserted the army. It had disgraced the family, and the town's condemnation had forced us to leave Tiverton.'

'I'm so sorry... that's why you lost contact with John.'

'Yes... and I don't think it helped having a different surname... Oh well, he would have found some exceedingly beautiful lady and settled down, I'm sure. He had all the girls trying to snap him up!'

I smiled.

She stood up to return the letters to the cabinet when I quickly intervened, 'I would *love* you to read one, Joan...'

'You would?' She could hardly contain her happiness! She nestled back down contently in the chair. Opening a letter carefully, she started to read.

"*My darling Joan,*

It has been raining here all day. The food is not too bad, and today, I had a tin of peaches, which I relished with delight after the muck I've been eating to keep us alive. I took myself to the cinema last night, but the film wasn't great, couldn't understand the language. The boys and I have a game of cards each Monday, which we do enjoy.

How are things going with you? I do miss you, Joan and a good brew. We received news of the weather in Blighty, at least you had a decent summer.

I often recall those days when we were at the beach. Your beautiful laughter always captivated me. How can a man not love a girl like you? Your love brightens my day.

I enjoyed being with you every second of every day that we spent together. I need you more than my heartbeat. I love everything about you. I love who you are! I am happy you are mine. You're my reason to keep on living, my reason to fight this war, the reason why the world needs a future.

When I first met you, I couldn't believe my eyes. You blew me away and still have that effect on me as I write this from my tent.

Remember the last day we met before I was stationed to leave? I loved holding you, kissing you. I will always remember your frisky smile. I wiped your sad tears away with my never-ending kisses. Oh, Joan, how I miss you! The war must end one day, and should this war snuff one of our candles out, may it take us both, so we can be together forever.

I have your picture with me everywhere I go. It gives me hope that I will see you again soon and keeps me sane in the hard graft.

Forever yours, forever mine.

All my love,

JP"

+ + +

Having left in good time to catch my bus back, I ended up facing a ten-minute wait in the cold. It was getting late and the frigid air was cutting through my open jacket so I quickly buttoned it up and pulled the collar over my ears. Still freezing, I decided to try my luck with a brisk walk to the next bus stop wishing I had brought my gloves. The walk gave me time to think. *I wonder if John's still out there somewhere? Did he make it back from the war?* I love a good mystery, and the desire was captivating. *Could I find John Pollock? Surely I've got enough details from Joan to give it a go?* There was something compelling and romantic about it.

When I arrived home, it was lovely and warm. I saw the light on in Nan's bedroom. It was 9.00pm. I knew she wouldn't go to sleep until she knew I was home. She always was sweet like that.

'I'm back, Nan,' I called softly, 'love you!' Then I went straight to my room. After settling down I embarked upon online research. There were many John Pollocks! Overwhelmed, I wondered where to start. I pulled my revolving chair closer to the desk in reach of a pen and paper.

In the stillness of my bedroom, the question arose… Should I ask Nan's God for help? But then again, why would He even help me if He could? I supposed I had nothing to lose.

I closed my eyes and prayed firmly, 'OK God, if you are who Nan says you are, help me find John Pollock.'

Nan often said, 'Nothing is impossible with God by your side.'

That night, as I slept, I had the strange feeling that God had heard my prayer. *Would He do anything about it?* Well, in any case, my sleep was peaceful and serene.

+ + +

I spent months looking for John Pollock. For some reason all the Services I telephoned were extremely helpful and passed me on to an agency if they were not able to assist. I thought it would take me years, not months! That was the strangest thing… and I sensed God had something to do with it.

Emily was funny, as she knew I was helping Joan. She said, 'Mummy, is pollocks a fish in the ingwish channel? I had a dweam about them dancing and it was so floppy and silly!'

I had to laugh as it would have been impossible to find that 'fish' in the English Channel.

There were countless John Pollocks and I didn't know if he had a middle name which made the search harder. I eventually located five John Pollocks who were alive. They all lived in a radius of three hundred miles and one in Guernsey. I hoped one of them was Joan's lover. Nervous and excited at the same time, I telephoned all the numbers I was given, hoping one would be positive news.

I dialled the first number... 'Hello, I'm looking for John Pollock who lived in Tiverton in the 1930's... a friend of mine knew him and since the war has not heard from him. Are you able to assist me please?... Yes I have his details...'

'Oh, he's not on your system. Are you sure? Ok I understand.'

Well, on to the last number. Crunch time, I guess...

'Hello, my name is Collette Jukes and I'm trying to find a gentleman who was in World War II. Are you able to help me please? Yes, his details are...'

'Yes I can send my identification to you, not a problem. Can you give me two minutes...'

'I'm glad you received my ID. Are you able to now give me the information for my friend? Thank you so much.'

'What did you say? He's... he's... on your system... are you sure it's him?'

'Yes all the details I gave you are correct.'

My tongue temporarily paralysed by the news. 'Yes, yes I'm here. I'm... I'm...' joyful tears streamed down my ecstatic face as I hugged the phone against my chest. Joan's lover had been found, and he was alive!

'Yes, I'm here, sorry. He's where? ...how long has he been there? I understand. I will phone the nursing home. I don't know how to thank you!'

I phoned the nursing home and explained the situation.

I had found him!

Elation ripped through me. I danced in my room, as if in some jazzy dance competition, punching the air in jubilation. I couldn't wait to visit Joan and tell her face to face...

Guernsey had been occupied by Germany during World War II and John was a prisoner of war, forced to build fortifications for the occupiers. That could have been a reason why he had stopped writing to Joan and why Joan's letters ceased to be forwarded to him. John and his brother were stationed in Guernsey.

After the liberation, even though he tried to find Joan, his brother had wanted to stay in Guernsey and John had nothing to bring him back to England. He wasn't sure what had happened to Joan – he was unsuccessful in his many attempts to find her. He didn't know whether she had died in the war or met someone else.

+ + +

The next day when I arrived at Joan's house, she welcomed me into her tiny living room where I observed the bundle of letters on top of the cabinet. I stood before her and blurted out the wonderful news. She stared at me bewildered. Her heart didn't dare to hope.

'Whaa... what di...d you say?' she asked, shocked.

'I said I've found your John Pollock!'

For a moment, she stood stunned.

'I located John after months of research and phoning different agencies. He is in a nursing home in Guernsey. I called the nursing home and told them your story. I managed to speak to someone later who is his carer and John has told them all kind of stories and… stories of you. He talked about the foxtrot lady with the orange dress.'

'John! He's alive.' Her jubilant face said it all.

'My God has answered my prayers! My God has answered my prayers!' she shouted triumphantly, with her face turned heavenwards and her hands clasped in prayer.

Joy danced through her heart and she swayed gently from side to side.

'My John is alive, after all these years! My John, my John…' She wept, raising her hands in awe.

She enveloped me in a warm embrace, tears full of love in her eyes. Holding me like a mother holds a lost child, firmly, longingly, and lovingly. I couldn't stop my own tears from spilling over like a satisfying fountain on a summer's day as her love poured into me.

What thoughts must have rippled through her mind? The love stories she had recounted, the love letters from John, had suddenly come back to life. What a moment… I shared her immense joy.

Joan had a huge smile on her face as she pointed to the cushioned chair next to hers.

'Collette, dear, will you please sit with me?'

Smiling, I settled into the seat and wiped my smudged mascara.

Joan leant her head gently against the back of the sofa. 'All my life, I have been praying to God that he would send me someone to find my John. And here you are!'

Joan pulled a coloured tissue from a box on the table next to her. She swiped at her eyes and nose then gathered a shaky breath. Her gaze fixed on mine.

'I don't think it was by accident that you helped me months ago when I had the incident in the street. I believe God put you there at the right time. Thank you with all my heart for finding my John.'

Turning her eyes towards heaven she said, 'Thank you, Jesus.'

I smiled and nodded in acknowledgment. *Had God brought me to Joan? The prayer I had made to find John Pollock… He answered it?*

Excitedly, I gave Joan all the details. By the end of recounting the long tale, I had quite forgotten what she said about God bringing me to her.

+ + +

A few days later, Joan telephoned me. 'Collette, dear, how are you?'

'I'm doing good.'

'I wanted you to know that I've connected with the nursing home John resides at with the number you gave me. I told them that I wanted to surprise him.'

I was smiling inside, 'How wonderful Joan, I'm so happy for you. When do you travel?'

'In two weeks' time.' I heard the cheerfulness in her voice. 'I've already bought my plane ticket.'

'You must tell me all the news when you return!'

'You know I will. Bless you my dear Collette and… thank you from the bottom of my heart.'

+ + +

I learnt the story of Joan's visit to Guernsey in great detail – she loved to retell it. The taxi from the airport drove her directly to the hotel, which was located within walking distance from the nursing home where John lived.

Dressed up in John's favourite colour (at least it was in the 1930's!), orange; she wasted no time and walked to the nursing home with her handbag across her body, and spotless hat on her head.

A Receptionist led Joan to John's room, where a nursing aid was assisting him. She could hardly contain her excitement. 'Thank you, dear... Oh, I just can't wait to see him again!'

Joan's dulcet voice reached John's ears and caused him to stir and smile wistfully just as she entered the room. Although he did not recognise her appearance – they had both changed so much – she could still recall the creases of the smile she had fallen for. She came beaming towards him.

'Young Mr Pollock,' she said with irony, repeating a line from long ago, 'all the girls are jealous to dance with you, Miss Seaton not least of all.' She fumbled in her handbag and brought out the watch. He glanced at it and raised his eyes, glowing with happiness of recollection and realisation.

'Hello John,' she spoke tenderly, 'I'm your Joan.' Tears of joy brimmed in her worn eyes as she handed him the watch.

Breathless and bewildered, he could only murmur quietly, 'Jo... Joan... my Jo... Joan?'

He straightened up. His creased face, like a withered flower, began to bloom with new life. Thin lips quivered with inexpressible joy. His sweetheart's voice thrilled him. A stronger beat revived his failing heart.

He sighed and smiled, the kind of smile that makes an angel in the throne room of heaven smile. John's glistening eyes twinkled, and his face blazed with glorious joy. He had given up on ever finding her but all the hope and longing came flooding back fulfilled.

He shook his head in disbelief as tears tumbled down his old face like rain on a brilliant summer's day. He couldn't believe that his old sweetheart was before him. Joan settled in the chair next to his, holding and caressing his hand. Both were lost in the wonder of unspeakable joy.

As they reclined, she felt the presence of God fill the room. Indescribable gladness filled this old couple who had waited for such a time as this.

+ + +

As a child, Nan would read me Bible stories before bedtime. *Where was the Bible my Nan had given me for my tenth birthday?* I had kept it for sentimental reasons. I opened it and began to read.

In a quiet way I knew God had touched my life. I sensed peace and a greater desire to know who He is. I soon started to read my Bible regularly, before I travelled to work each day. *Did God use me to help Joan?* She said she had prayed for years for God to bring her someone to help her find John. Suddenly, I remembered Joan's face as she told me I was the one God had brought to her. *Had God chosen me for this purpose or was it a coincidence?*

Over the months, my heart began to change. The Bible became more real to me as I read it. It truly was a love story – of God's love for me. My heart began to sing.

One day, I went to find Nan, who was sitting comfortably on the sofa knitting a new cardigan for Emily.

'Nan,' I blurted out, 'I want your Jesus too!'

Nan's face beamed. It was her look of loving pride in me that always made me feel treasured. 'I've been waiting a long time for this day,' she said as she placed her knitting down and ambled towards me, embracing me lovingly. Her eyes reflected the blessedness of my heart. My tears flowed freely. She brushed her aged fingers over them.

Nan knelt and I slid down upon my knees beside her in the L-shaped room. Holiness had engulfed the room. Nan reached gently for my hands and placed them readily into her beautiful, worn ones. A tear trickled from her closed eyes down her soft wrinkled cheek. In the silence, a gentle prayer was made to the God of heaven, and I asked to receive Jesus as my Saviour. A peace came over me that I had never experienced, a peace that only Jesus could bring and a peace that I could not explain.

REFLECTION

> No one can see the future, and Collette had no idea that she was about to help someone that needed a comforting hand the day of the incident. You and I do not know what lies ahead, but there is probably someone praying for us. Joan was praying to God to bring someone to find John Pollock, and Collette's Nan was praying for Collette and her great grandchild to come to know Jesus.
> Don't be surprised when Jesus touches your life. What you may think are coincidences in life may be God's hand in that situation.

WORDS OF WISDOM

You never know who is praying for you – or whose prayers you might be the answer to.

BOOK OF ESTHER

The Bible narrates the story of Esther, a young Jewish girl who married the King of Persia. Someone in the King's palace had plotted to kill all the Jews and secured the King's approval.

The King did not realise Esther, his wife, was a Jew. She was bold enough to speak to the King, requesting that he spare her people's lives. He did so; in a dramatic reversal, those who had tried to massacre the Jews were themselves killed.

The story asks, in the words of Esther's older cousin and adoptive father Mordecai, whether she was born *"for such a time as this"* (Esther 4:14 NIV) – that is, to save her people from annihilation. She didn't know that God had an assignment for her when she married the King, but in the end, it was her courage and wisdom that God worked through to save his people. I wonder what assignment God has for you!

REBECCA · JULIA · COLLETTE · AMBER
I'm Waiting For You

*"Ask and it will be given to you; seek and you will find;
knock and the door will be opened to you.
For everyone who asks receives, the one who seeks finds;
and to the one who knocks, the door will be opened."
(Matthew 7:7-8 NIV)*

Golden sunlight flickered in through the tilted blinds on a beautiful spring day. The window was slightly ajar and the gentle breeze danced with the delicate, sweet scent of the wild lavender on the window ledge as the chatter of shoppers and a low rumble of traffic happily passed by.

Julia's modern three-bedroom apartment nested above a colourful, stylish, boutique shop, owned by her parents. Her three friends, Amber, Collette and Rebecca, lounged comfortably in the cosy living room. The women had met on a Christian singles' holiday, five years ago, in Sicily and had kept in touch ever since.

Amber and Collette intentionally booked Christian holidays hoping to meet eligible Christian guys. What better place, other than church, to find a potential husband!

Several times a year, the women arranged an exciting weekend together. Julia lived in Islington, London, and had enthusiastically booked for them to watch the outstanding musical 'Miss Saigon' at the West End.

The friends chatted merrily through the warm morning, curled up on the bubble gum blue sofa, listening to Lucy Grimble's relaxing music swirling softly in the background. Collette glanced sideward at her friends from the open kitchen door, pouring coffee from the percolator. She took a biscuit from the plate on the work surface and happily gobbled it up, licking the crumbs from her full lips, whilst jigging to the music.

She called cheerily through to the lounge, 'Hey girlfriends, you'll never guess what happened to me!' She scanned the kitchen to see what else she could eat. 'A few of my work colleagues and I went sailing a few months ago. We were on this fancy yacht, right, for some team-building out on the water, they said. Anyway, I hadn't seen some from the other offices for such a long time, and I was so happy to see them. I leapt up and pulled them into my arms as they arrived.'

Grabbing a second biscuit and fresh coffee in hand, she came back in and continued, 'I was totally absorbed in the chit-chat, happily nattering away, and – get this – I hadn't even realised...' nibbling the biscuit, 'Louise my friend whispered, making these urgent pointed eyes at me. Couldn't make out what she was trying to say. Then the penny dropped... And would you believe it, my false ponytail had fallen off! Oh man... I went as red as a London bus, I was so embarrassed!' She carefully squatted on the floor crossed leg. 'There it was sprawled on the ground. I swiftly bent and retrieved it. Utterly embarrassed!'

The women guffawed vigorously, imagining the hilarity.

'Totally mortified, I reattached it to my head.' Collette finished the biscuit, 'I wanted to shake off any dust from the hair, but thought I'd better not and carried on the conversation as if nothing had happened.'

'Oh, my goodness, Collette!' howled Amber.

'Can you imagine how I was cringing deep inside?'

Highly amused, Julia chortled, 'Oh Collette, it's just like you to have something like that happen. I wish I was there!'

The happy chatter of the friends continued, as they shared their stories and their heartaches with one another. Although otherwise content with their current lives, the women shared one common whinge – they were all single in the love department, and had been for several years or more.

Strolling towards her armchair, Julia's attention was stolen by the peony flower petals. They basked in the sun on top of the glass table in the middle of the room... She sat down, distracted, but missed the chair and landed awkwardly on her rear, crying out in surprise.

After a brief pause in which her friends judged her to be uninjured, a fresh bout of laughter erupted. Julia laughed along to cover her embarrassment, brushing her dress down and stumbling up the chair. She whisked up her coffee cup and smiled with amusement as she shook her head. She gulped down the dregs of her coffee and rested back in the seat with a large smile, happy to be among friends.

Julia, a twenty-seven-year-old hotelier, had prominent hazel eyes which enhanced her olive skin tone. She wore a loose mauve cotton jersey dress, complementing her plus-sized physique. Previously, Julia had worked as a nanny. She adored the children she had cared for, even though it had been hard work tending to them and the spacious home. Her love for the children had given her a taste of motherhood and stirred her desire to have children of her own one day.

Her friends knew the heart-breaking tales of the disappointing ex-boyfriends. None of them seemed right for her. She wondered how long she would have to wait before God brought her a 'knight in shining armour,' preferably skinny jeans and a nice shirt, with one of those genuinely kind smiles! *Am I meant to be single for the rest of my days?* She wondered – and hoped not, she longed to be married and have children.

Meanwhile, seated on the floor with her back against the wall, was Amber, with her legs outstretched and crossed at the ankles. Amber was a medical secretary. She was a lovely woman with sparkling eyes that lit up her oval face as her flowing, hennaed hair tumbled gracefully around her shoulders. Never in her wildest imagination had she thought she would still be single at fifty-five.

Julia sighed aloud and put words to her aching feelings, 'Do you think I... *we'll* ever find that someone to share our lives with?'

Trying to keep her voice from straining, Amber reminded Julia, 'At least you've had boyfriends and have known what it's like to be accepted and loved by one, for a while.'

Her envy of those who had dated was still a sore point, while for the most part she tried not to get bitter. Although she was happy for them, she couldn't help but wish she had one too. She was looking for Mr Right and she didn't want to waste time dating someone who wasn't interested in marriage. And Mr Right needed to share her strong faith, which limited her selection.

A regular attendee at her local church, Amber loved socialising with other Christians and attending the weekly Bible study and prayer meeting. She used to regularly pray to God to give her a spouse and put her days of being a singleton behind.

She often wondered what was wrong with her. Amber had been waiting for so long; how much longer would she have to wait? A year, five years, ten years? It got frustrating sometimes. She desperately wanted a mate. The journey of her life had not looked how she had pictured it growing up. Had she already missed the opportunity to meet a husband? Most nights she whispered tenderly under her breath, 'I'm waiting for you… God will bring us together.'

'I do wish God would hurry up and send someone to me,' said Amber quietly.

'Patience is a virtue they say, but… it's hard,' echoed Rebecca adjusting her seating position.

Twenty-nine-year-old Rebecca worked for a digital marketing company. She was plain looking by the demanding standards of social media but had bright adoring eyes. Deep down, she wanted someone magnetic, but she had her fears. Years ago, she had fallen in love with a guy who had broken her heart. She had loved him, but he didn't love her.

Lying on her side, she remarked contemplatively to the others, 'Sometimes when you think you've found the love of your life, they let you down…'

There was complete silence.

'I don't know if it's better to be loved and have a heartache or not to be loved and be lonely,' resounded Amber.

Fluttering her eyes to stop the tears and propping herself up in a seated position Rebecca replied, 'I agree, I don't know which is more painful, to be loved and have a broken heart or not to be loved and never knowing what it's like… Maybe some women are meant to be single… including me,' she continued to sip the black liquid.

'I would love to have a guy in my life who is tall, dark and… sexy.' She pronounced the last word in a sultry voice and lingered on it.

Laughter filled the room – they could imagine the wheels turning in Rebecca's head and knew what she was getting at.

'I know in my head that God always provides like He provided a wife for Isaac in the Bible, so why hasn't He provided me with a man?' she lamented.

'Sometimes I feel like losing patience, big time! I so want to have children,' she sighed. 'In another ten years, I'd be over the hill… and far away.' She frowned, upset from thinking about it. She didn't want to be like Amber, still single at fifty-five. At least she had time on her hands, unlike Amber.

Collette, a forty-one-year-old single mother of a boisterous ten-year-old daughter was talkative and inquisitive, compassionate and kind, slender with kinky black hair and a chocolate complexion; she was a part-time solicitor.

Collette had had a few boyfriends, but none were worthy of settling down with. She wanted someone who would love her for who she was and love her daughter. She attended church services regularly and enjoyed participating in church events and Christian holidays. She loved sports and swam most days, always entertaining herself in a creative evening class and meeting new people.

'My friend Samantha Stringer,' Collette reminded the women, 'is over fifty and is still waiting for a hubby.' Collette couldn't fully understand why her best friend Samantha was still waiting. She had an attractive figure and a charismatic personality.

She wondered whether men thought attractive women were already taken or if some men weren't confident enough to ask such women out for fear of rejection. Collette often wondered if women should take the plunge and ask men out - and why ever not?

What was the hold-up? They knew perfect men did not exist, and neither were they perfect. Surely, there was a man out there for each of them?

'We all want to get married, don't we!' exclaimed Amber twisting her hair with a finger, as the women turned their attention towards her.

'Right,' chorused Julia and Rebecca, with Collette nodding profusely.

Rebecca sat up and wrapped her arms around her body. 'How I long for a man to put his arms around me,' she said playfully, 'and squeeze me tight and love me...'

Julia left her seat with outstretched arms and sauntered towards Rebecca, saying, 'I'll put my arms around you and squeeze you tight... my darling.' She chuckled as she leant down to embrace her friend.

'Seriously!' squealed Rebecca, as she too laughed in joy. She affectionately reciprocated the hug.

'I want a physical man not a man in some glossy magazine,' Rebecca continued as she pulled her knees against her chest in her trendy tight jeans. Julia strolled back to her seat, ears attentive as Rebecca continued, 'I want someone to kiss me, hold me,' she tightened the grip around her legs, 'go to bed with me at night and wake up together snug and warm... Someone to love and to be loved by... Someone who is not only a companion but a friend.'

'Isn't that what we all long for?' Amber said softly, 'The touch of a man? It's not just having a spouse, having fun in the bedroom and making babies,' her voice was comforting and uplifting, 'it's all the other things that go with marriage – love, intimacy, friendship, trust and the deep bond between two people.'

'One of the greatest temptations we face, being single, is our sex drive. Let's face it,' voiced Collette. 'That's one of many reasons I want to get wedded.'

Circling her head glancing at each of her friends one by one, Julia said, 'God made sex so we could enjoy it. Why should we miss out?'

'Sex is great, but it's not worth having sex before marriage. I know,' chipped in Rebecca, lowering her eyes as she ruffled her blouse sleeve.

'You're not alone Rebecca,' murmured Julia as her loving eyes met her friend's. 'Many Christian women and men have given into sex. As Christians, we believe we should wait to be married to have sex, but it's hard waiting. It's not easy… there have been times I've almost given in,' turning her face towards Collette.

'You have, Julia?'

'Yes, I have Collette… and it doesn't help being surrounded by a culture that devalues sex and tries to pretend it doesn't have any lasting impact on your heart or your body.'

Resting her chin on her knees, Rebecca gently replied, 'It's so true what you've said. God said it for a reason, even if I don't understand it myself. It's hard, but lots of good things are, like working hard to get an education.'

'Yes, it's hard...' Amber said as her gaze met Rebecca's. Their eyes locked in a shared understanding. Amber imagined how painful it must had been for Rebecca to be in a broken relationship and refrained from saying anything that would hurt her friend.

'Sex, sex, sex! None of us are getting it. How I desire it! How I long for it! I think I need a cold shower now!' Collette whined as the others laughed merrily.

'Sex in films is unrealistic. It's not available on tap and romance isn't round every corner,' huffed Rebecca.

'It's not just sex,' Julia remarked. Leaning against the arm of the chair, legs crossed at the knee. 'It's to love and be loved.'

Cheering each other up, the women agreed to make a list of the pros of being single. Julia merrily marched to her desk and grabbed a pen and a large notepad. Humming to the music, she flopped back in the chair.

'OK, what benefits of being single can we be thankful for?' She wrote down what the women said as they spent a laughter-filled morning on the list, until they had exhausted their ideas. Many cups of tea and coffee later, this is what they settled on:

BEING SINGLE AND ITS BENEFITS

- No mother-in-law
- Read whenever you want
- Go on holiday with your girlfriends without being questioned
- Never wait for the loo or shower
- Stay as long as you want in the shower
- Cook for one and cook anything you fancy
- Listen to music whenever you want and as loud as you want
- Clean when you want
- Wash the dishes when you want
- Burn the cooking and no snide comments
- Squeeze the toothpaste at the end or from the middle
- Have the whole bed all to yourself
- Wear anything to bed
- No one to hog the duvet
- Have full control of the remote (not in Collette's case!)
- More time to spend with your child
- You and your child get each other's undivided attention and love
- Learn to be independent, self-sufficient and develop new skills
- More time to spend with friends
- Avoid heartaches from relationship problems.

At times when the women felt lonely at home, they knew they could call each other and share their feelings. They knew they would be supported and cheered up, especially by Collette who tended to see the funny side of things and made them all laugh.

Famished, the women decided to eat out for lunch to celebrate their singleness.

They were thankful to have each other to lean on.

'You know, I'm so grateful to have you as friends. I had a great morning spending it with treasured friends,' Rebecca commented, 'to be loved, cherished and accepted for who I am.'

'Yeah!' yelled Collette, 'where would we be without each other.' As she placed her arm lovingly around Rebecca's shoulders.

'Where would we be without God!' smiled Julia as she reminisced… 'Remember the time I ended up in a police cell because I was high on drugs. Even there God was with me but I didn't know it at the time,' she continued.

Raising from her seat stretching her arms to the ceiling, Collette commented, 'I never guessed I would be helping an elderly lady find her lost sweetheart… I couldn't have done it without God.'

Amber interjected, 'God has a plan for all of us, I wonder what the next chapter of our lives would be?'

'I wonder too!' said Collette, smiling and tilting her head upwards to heaven.

'Come on Collette,' grinned Julia, 'Let's go. No doubt you're day-dreaming of your knight in... an Armani suit,' as the others joined in a merry laugh.

'Or could it be jeans and trainers,' chuckled Rebecca.

'Oh, shut up,' smiled Collette, 'there's nothing wrong in day-dreaming. Some dreams do come true!'

'Let's daydream of food,' said Julia as she and the others grabbed their bags to leave the apartment.

As Julia left to lock the door, she glanced at the list lying on the table. She ran back, found some tac and smiled as she pinned it to the inside door and locked the door happily behind her. She was glad that being single had its benefits.

WHAT ARE SOME REASONS FOR WOMEN BEING SINGLE?

This is always a sensitive area for many women because many who want to be married find that they're single for much longer than they expected. Some desire children, a natural feeling for most. Women can feel their biological clock ticking away. Some are constantly reminded about this, especially women who are in their mid-thirties or forties desiring to have a child.

This can cause anxiety, and the consequence of stress can leave single women weary and drained. Hormones also have a role to play in our desire for the physical affection and closeness of a man.

Women may have lists and are looking for all, if not some, particular qualities in a man. It's not wrong to have a list; I know people who have made lists and have received their answers. If you desire to make a list yourself, I recommend you take the time to ask God to give you His desires in your heart beforehand.

Some women feel wounded and need to experience healing, and to have the confidence to believe that they're lovable as they are, and yes they do have something to offer someone else. Our loving Father God longs to reverse our woundedness and to heal its root causes.

We're all familiar with the adage 'don't judge a book by its cover,' and indeed it might be a good idea to get to know a guy as a friend before making a judgement of whether to date him or not. Socialising with other Christians, for instance, Christian holidays, rambling clubs, volunteer work or reputable dating agencies are ways to meet others. Date for the right reasons, to love and be loved.

It's easy to quote, "But those who wait on the Lord, shall renew their strength; they shall mount up with wings like eagles, they shall run and not be weary, they shall walk and not faint" (Isaiah 40:31 NKJV). When we're faced with disappointments, these words can come across as over optimistic or dismissive – but Isaiah was no stranger to suffering and lament, and there is great wisdom and comfort to be found in the call to wait on the Lord and trust in Him. "Trust in the Lord with all your heart, and lean not on your own understanding. In all your ways acknowledge Him, and He shall direct your paths" (Proverbs 3:5–6 NKJV).

REFLECTION

> Do you identify with Rebecca, Julia, Collette or Amber?
> At times, do you get frustrated and almost lose hope? What helps you keep going?
> Are there any blockages on your side of the equation that you can start to take down? What help do you want from Father God?

It's wonderful to be romanced and in love but it's not the cure for being single. Our culture idolises romantic and - especially - sexual relationships, but our relationships with friends and family can also be very significant and meaningful, and of course our relationship with God can be the closest of all.

While you're waiting on the Lord to bring you a husband, why not pray for him. Maybe he is already praying for you! Let me also emphasise, it's ok to make mistakes - it's okay to date someone and realise it's not the right direction for the two of you. Indeed, a prospective marriage couple probably need to create enough rapport that they can discuss big important questions like 'do you want to marry one day', 'do you want children one day', 'do you want to adopt', 'is your dream to emigrate to another country'; and to start to find compromises to any number of other issues like 'would we live near your parents or mine' or 'do you want to keep pets?' Always good to know what you both want before committing to marriage.

It's so easy to go out with a guy and end up getting married out of desperation or even marry a man and think 'I can change him,' because we don't want to be alone. The marriage may work, but you probably will not be happy with such a compromise. It's better to be single and wanting to be married than married and wanting to be single.

Some people are called to live single, celibate lives - as were Jesus and Paul - and that is a valid and fulfilling way to live. Paul even suggests (in 1 Corinthians 7:7) it might be better, if you are called to it, to be single. If you are called to be single God will give you the strength (see Philippians 4:13).

A call to singleness might not be mutually exclusive with the call to become a mother, as single people are eligible to adopt, and there are many children who need a loving home.

If you are married or settled into a life of singleness how might you be able to sensitively support those who are seeking to be married?

WORDS OF WISDOM

Ladies, if you have a desire for a man, in your life, the likelihood is that God has one for you. So, what's the holdup? I cannot answer that question, but what I can advise is to tell God how you are feeling.

Why not write God a letter? Like you would write a letter to a friend, why not write one to God and let Him know exactly how you are feeling. Sometimes we can surprise ourselves as we write and discover feelings we didn't know we hadn't expressed, or gain a new perspective on things that we had only said short, rushed prayers about before. It doesn't matter how short or how long a letter to God is.

Here are the letters each of the women in this chapter would write:

Dear God,

Can you hurry up and give me a husband.

Thank you.

Julia.

+ + +

Dear Father,

I know I'm not perfect and I don't claim to be. Thank you that Jesus died not only for my wrong doings but also my mistakes. Father, I have made so many mistakes. I bring them all before you now and lay them at the foot of the Cross. Thank you for allowing me to do that.

You already know what I'm going to ask before I even ask you. I so want a husband, Father. You made Adam, and saw it wasn't good for him to be alone and you gave him Eve. Father, you can see it's not good for me to be alone. I don't feel good being alone. I'm not asking for an Adam who is incredibly handsome and perfect in every way, but I'm asking for a man who loves you and will love me.

Thank you. I love you,

Your daughter,

Amber

+ + +

Dear God

Thank you for being God and that you are able to do anything.

I'm not used to writing letters especially to someone as awesome as you.

You made me with desires for a hubby. Yet I'm still single. I'm not sure why?!

Can you bring me a man please... like now. I've read in the Bible that nothing is impossible with you. I will trust you.

From

Collette

+ + +

Dear God,

If you want me to be single please take this desire away from me.

Rebecca.

REBECCA
Never Too Late

"'For I know the plans I have for you," declares the Lord,
"plans to prosper you and not to harm you,
plans to give you hope and a future."'
(Jeremiah 29:11 NIV)

Five long years had passed since my relationship with Carl had shattered, and my heart with it, when the unthinkable happened. Never in a million years had I dreamt that I would experience something so unimaginable...

I attended my local church regularly, but only out of duty. My dedication to church had dwindled, and I mainly went there to chill with friends. I didn't feel any inkling of desire to visit my church, and I was certain God didn't want me there either, considering my past mistakes.

I wasn't happy with life, and, for years, I wore a mask for every occasion – I'd go hiking with friends with my sporty smile on; I'd go bowling, and promptly plaster my game smile on. Deep down, however, unimaginable misery flooded my soul. Yet, no one knew the inner storms with which my soul had been grappling. I had become skilled at hiding my agony. Who would have thought I nursed such deep secrets? Secrets that would only bring me shame if, God forbid, anyone came to know about them. Often I wondered, *how long can I keep playing charades before the wall cemented around my heart starts to crack?*

+ + +

Sunlight beamed in through an open window of the cosy coffee shop where Patricia and I were casually lounging, chatting amidst the pale green walls and mahogany tables. I removed my cardigan and welcomed the cool breeze of the ceiling fan, blowing through my thin cotton dress. We were sat across from each other, nestled comfortably in a corner booth, and waiting hungrily for lunch and feasting on the smells of fresh coffee and cooking.

Like me, Patricia leaned back and removed her summer jacket, revealing smooth, bare arms. The calm lavender jacket matched her elegant trousers. She reached decisively for my clasped hands and held them tightly within her soft manicured ones. On my wrist was the gold-beaded chain bracelet that she had bought for me as an engagement present. She gazed at it adoringly.

'Rebecca,' she gently murmured, 'no matter what it is that's hurting you, I am here for you and will always be. "God heals the broken-hearted and binds up their wounds."' The pain rose in me again. Despite the love and kindness in her tone, or maybe even because of it, she was dragging it all back to the surface. We exchanged faint smiles, and I inhaled her citrus perfume.

Patricia Bishop, my sister-in-law, was a kind and caring woman. She was a Christian blessed with good judgement, intelligence, and maturity. My brother, Darren, and Patricia were ministers in a thriving church in Cambridge.

When she attended my home church as a visiting speaker with my brother, I couldn't help but observe how her compassion-driven interactions with people, especially the sick and deprived, and her overwhelming love for lost souls were admired by all. She was faithful and honest in all her endeavours.

Darren was ten years my senior. I was the youngest, and our sister Ruth was the middle child. We grew up in Somerset, and I, for one, continued to stay there well into my adulthood. Ruth lived in Folkestone with her family, and Darren resided in Cambridge, along with Patricia and their two small children.

Patricia had met Darren at Spurgeon's Theological College, where both had been studying to be full-time ministers. It was their eighth year of ministering to their congregation, and they had come home to Somerset for a month of their three-month sabbatical.

Patricia quickly discerned, during the first week of her stay, that I had been hiding something. I had read in the Bible, "The eye is the window to the soul." I can admit now that it scared me when Patricia perceived my truest, most authentic self.

'You've always been special to me, like my own sister,' and she continued, 'I love you.'

I shuffled uneasily in my seat. My throat tightened and dried. My eyes watered. The roots of my parched heart strained for the refreshing consolation of her words. My voice croaked.

'Can we, err, go somewhere quiet where we can maybe talk, after lunch?'

'Sure,' she politely responded, but the frown on her slender face showed her concern. I quickly averted my eyes and pretended to inspect the floral wallpaper.

Quickly finishing our lunch, Patricia slipped on her jacket as I carried my cardigan. We then drove away from the neighbourhood.

'Do you remember Spiral Baptist Church?' Patricia asked.

'Yes, of course, where Darren took you to the youth meetings when you were dating?'

'That's the one,' she smiled, 'Do you remember the beautiful gardens? I know a side entrance – I'll show you.'

It was nice to feel whisked away – I couldn't remember the last time someone had valued me like that. I could feel the care in her smile. Here was the simple care of friendship with no strings attached. Oh, how I'd missed it!

In the garden, an enchanting floral scent lingered in the air, and this blessed closeness to nature rejuvenated me. Patricia and I sank next to each other on the bench, near a bed of pink, yellow and red roses. We were alone, apart from the birds chirping in the trees and bees hovering from flower to flower gathering nectar. A colourful butterfly danced near my head. I watched as it settled on the flower beside me, as if eager to hear me speak, encouraging me with a gentle open and close of its wings. Intrigued, I watched it until the breeze carried it away.

Patricia untied her shoelaces, took off her heels and placed them carefully to one side of the bench. I watched, amused, as she rested her dainty feet on the cool grass. As she slowly directed her piercing gaze towards me, I remembered why we had come. My palms became clammy. My heart pounded with every beat.

'Patricia,' I forced the words out, 'you know Carl and I broke up?'

'Sure, I thought everyone knew,' she said, puzzled, as she brushed away soft curls of hair falling on her neck.

Blushing, I dropped my gaze. I glanced up, stealthily, to check her response. I was hesitant and nervous about what she would think of me. However, I took a deep breath, and in a moment of sudden peace and clarity, I replied, 'No one knew we had an intimate relationship.'

She leaned over and caught me in her grass-green eyes. 'Is that what has been eating you up?' she asked tenderly, studying the worry lines etched in my expression.

'It's part of it,' I feebly responded blushing. 'It wasn't a one-off… I.… I had been intimate with Carl for,' inhaling deeply, 'I don't know… months. Then he broke me, I mean, broke up with me without any explanation. N-nothing!' Tears welled up without warning, like rain gate-crashing a summer picnic, and I rapidly swept them away with my fingers. Patricia opened her bag and took out a pink handkerchief as I continued sniffling.

'I think I'll need more than a handkerchief!' I exclaimed, and, for a moment, we both exchanged smiles. I fussed with the handkerchief on my lap.

Just then, a golden beam of sunlight broke through. I hadn't realised the sun had tucked itself away behind a cloud until then, and the warmth of the glorious light was an unexpected comfort.

'Patricia, you have no idea what it has been like for me. To this day, I… I… don't know what… what did I do? Why did he… why did Carl feel so compelled to… to… leave me!'

She leaned her bare arm behind me on the top of the bench, 'Hey, it's OK… Did you try to get an answer from him?'

I tilted my head from side to side, 'Yes, but... he wouldn't open up. He shut me out.' I stared ahead and blinked to find composure – the last thing I needed was a fresh rain of tears.

'All he said was... he was sorry and... and goodbye. I did speak to Mum about it but, as you can understand, I couldn't... I just couldn't... go into too much detail. I... I hate him,' I said narrowing my eyes. 'Urgh, Carl! It hurts so much!' My bitterness burst its banks. Quickly, Patricia squeezed my hand. She was no stranger to heartache.

Patricia was engaged to be married, fifteen years ago. On the day of the wedding, she waited at the church for her groom, who never showed up. All the guests were there, and reservations for the honeymoon had been arranged, they even bought a house together. I can't imagine what she must have gone through. Yet all bitterness had evaporated and she shone love.

'Hey, I'm here for you,' she assured me softly, 'I understand.' Her warm eyes welled with tears. 'We all want to be loved, and... you loved Carl unreservedly.'

Lowering my eyelids, I confessed, 'Yes, I did. I loved him too much for my own good.'

'Love poisoned by pain can turn to hatred,' Patricia said sadly. I could feel her gaze, or maybe it was the sun. 'Do you hate him because he left you?'

I fidgeted. I struggled to speak. No words could escape my choked throat. I was on the verge of tears, again, and my eyes strained from side to side. I nodded, and, before I could control my emotions, I erupted, 'I hate him because he made me feel worthless. Because he used me – he used me! He threw me away with a pathetic 'sorry'! I hate him... I do, I do...'

Bowing my head, I broke down. Half a decade of anger raged inside me. My contorted face laid bare my pain. She encircled me with both arms and clasped my shoulder tightly.

'Let it out, Rebecca, let it out... I'm here for you.' Crying with me, her body jerked against mine.

'People can be so cruel,' she said tearfully, 'but God never leaves us, never abandons us, never uses us, Rebecca, and always loves us, loves us so completely. That's what got me through when Matthew left me.'

Wiping my tears, I sputtered, 'He rejected me – made me feel like a trash bag dumped out on the street, as if none of it had mattered... and I felt so betrayed. Carl devastated me.' Once happy memories of his touch and laughter, long-since soured, flooded back. Gasping for breath, I sobbed, 'I loved... him... He hurt me so much. I... I... loved him.' I buried my tear-streaked face in her shoulders.

Although I had been reticent about my personal affairs, I knew I had to tell her the full story. The vulnerability was biting.

The thought of disclosing this burden on my heart was excruciating; my very bones ached, but I trusted her.

'There's… there's more, Patricia.'

She gently leaned out to study my face, stroked my shoulder and whispered, 'Do you want to tell me?'

I glanced at her over my shoulder. I was heavy with shame. I knew Patricia was pro-life, which made it all the more difficult for me to open up… my hands shook as an earthquake inside cracked and tore at the cemented walls around my buried heart. After a moment of hesitation, I whispered my confession, 'I had… an abortion.' I gasped for the breath I hadn't realised I was holding.

My shoulders heaved up and down, like a boat battered by waves, pouring out every ounce of emotion that had been buried inside me for so long.

Anguished, she exclaimed, 'Oh, my sweet Rebecca! How did you bear this pain all alone?'

I strained for words, I felt as if my innermost being was being ripped away; as if I was dying inside, just like after I had the abortion.

'I know you're pro-life... Do you... do you think less of me? I so wanted to talk to someone... I couldn't trust anyone enough to confide in them. The shame felt just so... sickening inside.'

She held me tightly and allowed me to weep away my sorrow. She continued to embrace me all the while until my sobbing subsided. Although I felt safe in her arms, I was anxious because this was only a small part of this painful story. *Should I tell her the rest? What will she think of me?* I hesitated. *Will she reject me?* I didn't want to be rejected again. *Is she ready to hear what had happened after the abortion? Will she be ashamed of me?* I worried. But my dam had burst, and I realised that the time to hide behind my pain was long over. I took a plunge of faith into the rushing waters and decided to reveal everything.

'I blamed Carl for the abortion, and I told him so. I struggled every day, knowing the baby was no more, and I blamed him, and I still do.'

She studied my wounded eyes, frowning with concern. 'Did it make you feel better when you blamed Carl?'

I said bluntly, 'No.'

'Do you think God stopped loving you because of what you did?'

My eyebrows lowered and pulled into a grimace. 'Yes,' I said firmly, even though my chest was quivering.

'I can assure you He didn't. His love for you never faltered in any way, Rebecca. He is a good, good Father. Even when a child does wrong, the mother doesn't stop loving the child. Why would God stop loving you? He feels your pain with you. His heart breaks with yours,' she placed her hand over her heart. 'Hate is like a festering wound, which doesn't heal, Rebecca, no matter how much you nurse it. Like a scab – pick it, and it gets worse. But there's always a way out.'

I fixed my eyes on her and exclaimed, 'A way out? I can't bring the baby back!'

'I know it feels overwhelming right now… where you're going is what matters, not where you've been.'

I bowed my head, leaning forward, preparing myself for the next confession. 'The story doesn't end there, Patricia.'

She raised her eyebrows, her empathetic eyes probing me. My red eyes locked with hers.

'God is not harsh,' Patricia said. 'He already knows what we will do before we even do it and still loves us… When Matthew didn't turn up for our wedding nothing prepared me for that day. I was as shocked as the guests but the pain was left with me not them. They had no idea what I was going through. They felt for me, but I was the one in pain, shame and despair.'

'But you went to his wedding?' I asked.

'Yes, I did,' she murmured, hugging her knees. 'About six months after our wedding date he contacted me. My first reaction wasn't great, I was angry and hurt, but I wanted to know why he did what he did. We met, and a lot of pain on my part came out. We didn't kiss and make up, but that helped me greatly – speaking to him helped me move on in my life. He kept in touch with me – not regularly, it would have been too painful. I was invited to his wedding four years later, but I got married to your brother first!' A big smile exploded on her face.

'How do you feel now?' I tentatively asked.

'I had to let go. Of course, it took time, years, but now I can say all hurt and bitterness has gone.'

'Rebecca, God is a loving and forgiving God. The Bible says, "If we confess our sins to God, He is faithful and He will forgive us our sins and cleanse us from all unrighteousness." If you seek his forgiveness and you mean it with your heart, He will forgive you. Don't let something in the past define your present.'

A tear slowly cascaded down my cheeks and landed on my lap. I leaned back against the bench, looking at the sky, fiddling with the handkerchief, and started to reveal the full, ugly story...

'After my relationship with Carl ended, everything felt hollow... I became so depressed. After the abortion, I was out of my mind with guilt so I learnt to bury it. Seeking a semblance of companionship to numb the pain, I started drinking and clubbing with people I met online, from the east side of Somerset. My family assumed I was going out with Christian friends, and I never told them otherwise. I kept getting drunk, and one day I got so drunk that I nearly drowned in my vomit... it was so horrendous that I quit cold-turkey... I felt so empty.'

'Is that why you didn't drink when your sister Ruth, had her thirtieth birthday?'

I inhaled sharply, 'Yes, that's right. As you know Ruth loves a cocktail and I had a desire to drink but, no way! After what I'm going to tell you, you'll understand why I became a teetotaller...' I looked at my sandals, mesmerised by the peace of this silence. Patricia waited patiently and whispered a prayer. All the while, I continued to battle through the tears.

'I know I had been blackout drunk, as the following morning I woke up in a stranger's bed. I have no idea how I got there. I didn't even know who he was! I realised then that my life was a wreck.' I glanced at my feet as I shuffled them.

Patricia placed a gentle hand on my lap. A flock of twittering birds flew overhead, as if to cheer me up.

I braced myself and continued, 'As I lay in bed, drowsy, and my head pounding as if someone was constantly hammering it, a man strolled towards me and peeked at me and asked, "How did you sleep?" I was aghast and jolted upright, pulling the bed covers closer to my chin. I was tongue-tied.

'He was pleasant and offered to drop me home. I asked him where I was. He replied, "You're in Weymouth, Dorset," he clarified after my blank stare, I wasn't even in Somerset! I didn't know his name and had to ask him. It was Ethan, by the way.

'He tried to persuade me to eat something and get to know him better. My head was thumping so hard, I refused vehemently. It was 11.30am. I asked him, "How did I end up there?" "By train," he replied matter-of-factly, as if nothing was wrong! I had no recollection whatsoever of boarding a train. "Did I get a return ticket?" I asked him. He laughed amusingly, but I failed to see the humour in it. I dressed hurriedly, grabbed my bag, and left without a goodbye. I didn't take in the street name or flat number.

'I marched down the streets and caught a bus that was approaching; it took me straight to the train station. I was so guilt-ridden, I felt so dirty, I put my foot down and decided that I would no longer drink. My life had gone from one whirlwind to another. I screamed at myself, *How could a Christian girl get so low? What was I thinking?!* Although I didn't know how, I knew I had to get my life back on track and crawl out of this mess.'

My voice rose an octave higher. 'This wasn't the life I wanted to live – shallow and empty! Do you think it ended there? No! It didn't, and the worst was yet to come. Never in my imagination did I think this would have happened to me.

'Oh, I was so good at pretending it wasn't happening, playing my part as the 'pure church girl' seamlessly!

'Not long after this, err, *encounter* with Ethan, I began putting on weight. At that time, I was just binge-eating to forget the past then I got violently sick. "It has to be a stomach bug," I told Lisa, my housemate. But it wasn't that simple – I was pregnant, again!'

Patricia pressed lightly on my hand. I hung my head in shame, but I knew I had come too far to back out now. I had to tell her the rest.

'My physician confirmed the pregnancy and warned me that I was too far gone to have an abortion. I was shocked because he told me the news without even conducting an extensive medical examination. Naturally, I wanted a second opinion, so I went to another clinic and they performed an ultrasound, and it turned out I wasn't too far gone. I was pregnant with twins!'

'Twins!' gasped Patricia, as she placed a hand on her chest. Although she tried to cover it up, I could see it was the same shock I too had felt back in the clinic.

'What... what happened?' Patricia asked, with palpable concern.

'I felt I was standing in the middle of a cyclone. I truly didn't know what to do. I couldn't have an abortion. I just couldn't go through with it again, not with two babies. I didn't know how to resolve this impossible dilemma. I couldn't be a mother, not to two babies, and not in the mess I was in.'

'You had the babies, didn't you?'

'Yes, I did.'

'What... what happened to them? You went away for a year to the North of England... You said you needed to clear your head... I thought it was because of Carl. You went away to have the babies?'

She was piecing the past together to complete the puzzle that my life had somehow turned into.

'Yes.' I hugged my arms across my waist. 'I never saw them... I couldn't. It was for the best.' My voice broke down, and I could feel each ounce of strength I had accumulated fading away into nothingness. 'I ensured they were adopted.'

'Oh, Rebecca, I only wish I could have been there for you.' Her voice was kind and composed. 'How do you feel about the babies now? I know it's none of my business, and I'll understand if you don't want to talk about it.'

'No, I'm glad it's in the open now,' I said meekly, smiling faintly. 'A loving family adopted them. The couple couldn't have children, so I was happy that my pain and guilt had contributed to a deserving family's life-long happiness. I knew they would be loved. It's still hard, though, knowing they are out there.'

'They are safe and loved. You did what you thought was best for them. You gave those two babies another life – a better life.'

'A boy and a girl.' We shared a pleasant smile.

'Can you remember what I said to you on your twenty-fifth birthday, Rebecca?'

I nodded. 'Oh yes, that year when it rained and rained. Yes, you said something like, "Never let something define you for the rest of your life if it's negative. Believe you are someone special and unique and God has a special assignment for you."'

'You remembered well.'

'There's more to my story.'

'More?' Patricia said in disbelief as she exhaled forcefully through her full lips.

'Yes, it doesn't end there.'

Her voice rose a semi-tone higher. 'What do you mean?'

'Even I had a hard time believing this happened to me.'

Frozen upright in her seat, Patricia listened intently.

'After I returned from the North, I wanted to close the chapter on the bunch of friends in the east of Somerset and bid them goodbye by seeing them in person. Some of them had been good to me, and one of them had even stayed connected with me while I had been away.

'On the day we arranged to meet, Ethan was there too. I was shocked initially, but I tried to keep a positive mindset, and we started chatting. In the end he seemed a nice guy, and we ended up going on a few dates… well, more than a few. I liked him, and he too was fond of me. But he had secured a job in France and would be moving shortly. Before he left, he told me how much he had enjoyed my company and felt disappointed that he was leaving.

'Considering everything that I had been through, I didn't know what came over me. I told him I had gotten pregnant *that* night. Like you, he was shocked and immediately began doubting me. I assured him it wasn't impossible. He said that had he known about the babies, he would have been a father to them somehow, and we could have worked something out. I was devastated at the loss of what could have been… the sadness in my heart was too much to bear.'

I stopped to inhale deeply, 'He was very kind and sympathetic towards me. It was as if he knew how rotten I felt inside. He said he was glad I didn't get an abortion. That encouraged me – at least I did something right!

'I told him that they had been adopted by a childless couple, and I had given the adoption agency the names of the babies, Ethan and Rebecca. He was joyful, yet sad, that I had named his son after him. I don't know if I did the right thing telling him that. But I thought, *Surely, he had a right to know?* We were getting on so well. We had a long chat, and I said it was best not to interfere and to leave the twins with the loving family.'

'Wow, Rebecca!' Patricia exclaimed, removing her sleeve-less jacket as small beads of sweat appeared on her brow, 'This is truly something! Are you all right?'

My lips curled into a smile, acknowledging her kindness.

'That was a huge decision you made, with no one supporting you, and it wasn't an easy decision either.'

I mumbled, 'No, it wasn't.'

'That is something I respect about you, your strength.'

'My strength?' I grimaced. I couldn't believe her praise, considering I had been admonishing myself for my actions for as long as I could remember.

'Yes, you must have incredible strength, considering you pulled through all of this alone.'

'I never thought of it that way.'

'You did what you thought best at the time, Rebecca. I'm glad I can be here for you now. My love for you hasn't diminished; rather, my admiration for you has soared. You shared your innermost heart with me, and I know it wasn't easy for you.'

'Wow, I never expected you to say that.'

Smiling, Patricia kindly responded, 'I will always be here for you… I love you.'

'You can't imagine how greatly you have encouraged me.' My eyes caught Patricia's comforting smile.

'Do you think… do *you* think Rebecca, Jesus can help you?'

Pondering… 'I knew Jesus could help people but I didn't believe he could help me. I wanted to be in control of my life. Clearly, I got it wrong. I questioned whether I could be a… a real Christian… when I was living life this way.'

Clasping my hands against my chin as my elbows perched on my thighs, I asked, 'Do you think God will truly forgive me for all my sins? Or is it too late to be saved?'

'Oh, Rebecca, it's never too late for anything with God.' Her eyes lighting up. 'Jesus did away with our blemishes. He died in our place so that we could be forgiven. If you are truly sorry, yes, He will forgive you for anything. He loves you and has never stopped loving you. Remember, Jesus died to forgive you for everything you've ever done wrong.'

'It's hard to comprehend,' I said. 'I have lived in a dark place and worn masks for so many years.'

'It's very hard to comprehend Jesus' death and resurrection. He rescued us from the power of darkness and escorted us safely into the kingdom of His dear Son.

'God chose you, Rebecca, with all your fractures. He chose you. He wanted you. He knew from the beginning what would happen, and He still wanted and loved you!'

She was so enamoured by Jesus' love I thought she was going to fly off her seat!

'Just because you took a detour doesn't mean that God has abandoned you. He will still honour you. If you only knew what God has been doing behind the scenes, knew how He is working out His plan for your life and fighting battles for you!'

I closed my eyes and was silent for a while, digesting her comforting words and imprinting them into my mind so that I could seek solace from those words in the future.

The church garden reminded me of God's wonderful creation. It made me reflect on how He cares for the little things even the birds of the air and the colourful butterflies, to the grass in this openness. I was thankful for life and the life of my twins. I realised God was saying, it's never too late.

'I do regret sleeping with men and going through with the abortion… I am happy the twins have a loving home now,' I said, as a tear slipped down my flushed face.

'Can I pray for you?' Patricia asked eagerly.

'Yes, please do,' I smiled.

Wholeheartedly, she uttered, 'Father, God, thank you for Rebecca, an incredible woman you created – a woman of beauty, strength and substance. I thank you that you know Rebecca's heart, and only you know what pain and suffering she has undergone, and how she is feeling right now. Please heal her heart, and mend the broken pieces in the way only you know how. In Jesus' name I pray. Amen.'

'Amen,' I echoed.

Turning towards me, she said brightly, 'Isn't it wonderful to know that Jesus died for our sins? He took them to the cross. We can just give them to Him, and He will reward us with joy and gladness.'

My heart sang with Patricia's words.

'Now, Rebecca, I think you know what you need to do. Be real with Jesus, as He already knows everything about you.'

I paused, bowed my head and truthfully said without any pretence, 'God, forgive me for my sins of sleeping with Carl and Ethan and for having the abortion. Please take away my shame, sorrow and inner pain and make me clean again. I release them all to you. Thank you for accepting them. Amen.'

'Is there something else you need to do?'

I frowned as I watched her for an answer, 'Like what?'

'Forgive Carl.'

I was flustered by the intensity of the question. Pressing my lips tight, I disdainfully declared, 'Never!'

'Remember God has forgiven you. Shouldn't you try to forgive Carl as well?'

'It's not as easy as it sounds,' I voiced, averting my eyes from Patricia's determined face. 'My heart is not ready to forgive him yet,' I said, folding my arms defiantly.

Leaning to the side, Patricia commented, 'Forgiveness doesn't necessarily take away the pain or undo the consequences Rebecca, but it loosens the grip of bitterness inside us and begins a path to healing. And on the journey, you might find you need to keep choosing to forgive over the same event. Forgiveness isn't fair at times. It's the grace that God gives us – something we don't deserve.'

'When you're ready, tell God what's in your heart.' Patricia gazed at the flowerbed. I noticed daisies pushing their way up through the overgrown grass. Miraculously, their cheerfulness and simplicity showed me God. The sun reflected off the church roof window resplendently. A bird sat on its steeple.

I folded my hands demurely on my lap. We were silent for some time. Silently weeping, I sank to my knees, and hot tears fell on the grass. 'God, you know how my feelings for Carl are. He hurt me so... so badly... the pain is still raw... He made me feel as if I were a rubbish bag being thrown out.' Clenching my hands tighter, I sobbed, 'Help me... please... to forgive him as you have forgiven me. In Jesus' name, Amen!'

Patricia slid off the bench and knelt on the grass beside me, 'Rebecca, God has heard your cry, and He has never abandoned you.'

I turned and smiled at her, 'Yes, I know. I thought He had because of what I had done, but I now realise that He was with me even when I was driving to the clinic.'

'Do you know He is here now with us?'

'Yes.' I replied as she reclined nearer to me.

'Rebecca as hard as it may be to hear these words - have you forgiven yourself?'

The bizarre question puzzled me. 'What do you mean?' I asked.

'God has forgiven you, so there is no need for you to torture yourself for past mistakes. Forgiving yourself simply means not holding your past wrongdoings against yourself anymore.' Her eyes fastened onto mine. 'As God has forgiven you, forgive yourself.'

I pondered. *Forgive myself?* It had never crossed my mind!

'Receive God's grace, Rebecca.'

'What do you mean?'

'God is rooting for us no matter what. If we fail, His loving arms are there to welcome us back, no matter how badly we have messed up. That's His grace – that's His love. Whatever we do, we cannot stop God from loving us or welcoming us back to Him.'

'I don't deserve God's love, I've done too much wrong.'

Patricia's voice full of compassion, 'That's what God's grace is, it's something we don't deserve. He was with you every time you cried yourself to sleep because He cares and loves you. Don't blame yourself Rebecca, forgive yourself, as God has already forgiven you... God has already forgiven *you*... when we don't forgive ourselves it's like a thornbush growing inside of us… God wants to take that thornbush away.'

Compelled by her tenderness and love for me, I bowed my head, 'God… how can I not blame myself for what happened… it was my decision… yet this grace of yours wants to take it all away as if it never happened… I don't deserve it… you love me that much?… forgive myself? I forgive myself for all the hurts I have inflicted upon myself. Please help me stop blaming myself and to see you don't blame me. Amen.'

Eventually, I lifted my head towards hers. Her unflinching love for me was evident in her eyes, which were brimming with tears.

'Rebecca, you've been through more than some people go through in a lifetime.' Her smile was warm and comforting. 'My sisterly love for you hasn't changed one bit because of your past. Again, I say I hold great admiration and deep respect for you, for being so brave by sharing your darkest secrets with me.'

Those words blew me away. I was amazed that she did not judge or condemn me. She saw my eyes widened with surprise.

'I remember how I felt when Matthew rejected me. I had a lot of hurt too. It was very painful. It will take time.' Patricia squeezed my hand.

'People say time is a healer, and how true it is. You'll get through it, with God's help.'

We embraced. I was so glad she was my family.

Patricia glowed knowing I received God's amazing love for me. I knew that day that Jesus had taken away all my sins, blame and mistakes. I received God's gift of grace to heal my heart. To my amazement, I felt so much lighter. How wonderful too that I had someone I trusted who knew the whole truth. The burden had been released, and I was at peace – with God and myself.

+ + +

Later that day, Patricia encouraged me to share the story with my mum. Patricia knew I shared a good relationship with my mum and thought, perhaps, now that it was out in the open, maybe it was time to tell her. However, she never pressured me.

Since the abortion, my relationship had changed between my Mum and myself. I think she sensed something wasn't right but thought it was the breakup with Carl. She did try to help me but I closed the door numerous times, because of the pain I was in and the fear that she might reject me. I couldn't face another rejection.

With Patricia's unwavering support, I bravely bared my heart to my mum during the week.

Hesitantly, 'Mum I have something to tell you...'

'What is it darling, are you alright?'

We had been standing in the small kitchen when I broke the news. She was aghast and lightly gripped her throat with her hand as her bosom heaved heavily. She lost her balance and held on to the kitchen table for support. The revelations came as a complete shock to her. She partly regained her composure and staggered towards me. Her strong embrace was comforting. However, I had mixed emotions. *Was she holding on to me for fear of falling or holding me because she knew how I was feeling?*

Then, laying all my doubts to rest, she smothered me with affection, caressing my hair like she used to do to reassure me everything was fine when I was a child. That's when I knew the depth of her love for me. What a release from the burden I carried by hiding it from the one who, I knew now, absolutely loved me. No more secrets.

Her warm tears rolled down my neck. We stood there in the kitchen and held each other tightly for what seemed like an eternity. She cupped my wet face in her delicate hands and looked intently at me with a loving smile, her eyes glistening with tears. She accepted me instead of reprimanding me. We strolled hand in hand towards the lounge and rested on the sofa. My mum's soft arm was wrapped around my shoulders, and I rested my head on her tender neck and eagerly delved into a long-awaited conversation with her.

'Mum, how I wish I had told you everything before.'

Cupping my face, 'Darling, don't worry, I'm glad you told me. What you must have been going through all these years.'

'I wanted to tell you but…'

'Shush… you've told me now and that's what counts. I love you Rebecca.'

A wide smile appeared on my face, 'I love you too Mum,' as we embraced each other with tears of joy.

+ + +

Last time I saw Patricia and Darren was at their farewell party at the church.

Patricia kept in touch with me every week, regularly dropping words of encouragement into my life, reminding me of who God made me to be and how He loved me, gently asking me to forget the past and strive for what lay ahead.

I had been in a dark place, insecure and vulnerable – ashamed of what I had done, what I had become and how unworthy I was. I had worn a mask so people couldn't see the real me. Underneath the mask, I had been afraid of rejection. I had pretended to be someone I wasn't. I had even pretended to be a Christian walking with God, to please my family.

I wrote a letter to God a year ago with my friends, and it said, 'God, help!' I didn't know what else to say. I now know He had heard and answered my prayers.

I was ready to get up and try again with God as my helper, my protector, and my friend.

+ + +

I cannot deny that I think of the twins and wonder what they are doing, I know eventually I will contact the adoption agency. I wouldn't want them growing up knowing I didn't want them to be part of my life.

I kept in contact with Ethan; he has moved on and is engaged, he too would like some kind of contact with the twins.

After a traumatic journey, who would have thought a new door would be opened to me. Presently, I have taken a job as a youth leader helping young people in my local church and sharing what God has brought me through.

I now see God as a Father whose love for me motivates His every action towards me. He is forever with me, wanting me to join Him in life's greatest adventures and joyfully enabling me to mature into everything He designed for me.

God is someone I can trust and look up to. He is someone I know won't judge me but will always be there for me. And He is someone I love and can call when I'm worried or in trouble.

I am thankful to God for how He has changed me, knowing it wasn't something I could possibly do myself.

REBECCA'S OWN WORDS...

God had blessed me immensely with a wonderful sister-in-law. I believe God brought her into my life at the right time to help me follow the Christian path once again. God, through Patricia, introduced me to His love and mercy. I learnt to lean on the Holy Spirit for truth and guidance. Slowly, but surely, I am learning much about God – He accepts me and truly loves me despite my past.

A friend of mine had once admitted with profound sadness that she had had nothing to look forward to when she had gotten married, not even the honeymoon, as she had been intimate with other men. Although I now regret what I did, I know the Father's healing hand is upon my life.

I may never marry, but I know that God is my husband and my best friend, who will always do whatever is best for me. He knows me and still loves me. If I do get married, I know feelings of guilt won't get in the way.

I am completely healed and free to be who God created me to be. I am cherished by an incredible family and, especially, the God of creation. No matter how far I wander, I now know my Heavenly Father will be waiting for me with forgiveness, love, and compassion like a parent, with arms outstretched, saying to a toddler, "Come to me, and I will give you rest."

REFLECTION

> Do you find yourself hurting because of how someone hurt you?
> Have you asked God to help you to forgive that person?
> Maybe you've had an abortion or given up a child for adoption. God still loves you.

HOW DID REBECCA SEE GOD?

Rebecca hadn't fully comprehended God's compassion and love for her as her Heavenly Father. "But God demonstrates his own love for us in this: while we were still sinners, Christ died for us" (Romans 5:8 NIV).

After laying down the heavy burden of her secrets, Rebecca was reminded of how Jesus had come to take away all her sins. She knew that she needed God's forgiveness because she had given her body to others when it didn't belong to them (see 1 Corinthians 6:19-20). She experienced God's love, forgiveness, and peace.

WHAT DID REBECCA DO?

She was ashamed of her past, and the secret was still there. Patricia introduced her to a compassionate, gracious, and merciful God. She saw God differently because of how Patricia portrayed Him in her life.

Is this why God brought Patricia into Rebecca's life to show her God's unreserved love? God may bring someone into your life or use another means to show you His love. God loves us.

It wasn't easy for Rebecca to let Patricia know about her past, but it was necessary. As we saw, her burden was lifted, she was released and her light could shine again.

Both Rebecca and Patricia prayed in the garden. It was a prayer of confession and forgiveness. We can ask God for forgiveness, which He bestows readily. We also have to forgive ourselves by letting go of the past. It's like blowing up a balloon, tying the end and letting it fly away – the balloon doesn't return.

"Therefore, repent and return so that your sins may be wiped away, in order that times of refreshing may come from the presence of the Lord..." (Acts 3:19-20 NASB).

"...The Lord, the Lord, the compassionate and gracious God, slow to anger, abounding in love and faithfulness" (Exodus 34:6 NIV).

WORDS OF WISDOM

'Lord, help me to be willing to let you change my heart to forgive.' Sometimes forgiveness is a process; it takes time. There is a story in the Bible of a man who asked Jesus how many times he should forgive someone and Jesus replied seventy times seven (Matthew 18:21-22). It may take time to forgive someone but ask God to soften your heart.

Forgiving others may be easier than forgiving yourself!

Prayer: Thank you, God, that you readily forgive me. Thank you it's never too late to come to you; you will never reject me, you always accept me. Thank you. Amen.

JULIA
The Telephone Call

"Let your hope keep you joyful, be patient in your troubles, and pray at all times."
(Romans 12:12 GNT)

Seven years had passed and Oscar and Bella were now independent teenagers. They no longer needed me as their nanny.

Their inspirational parents, who I adored, owned a chain of hotels, and had kindly offered me an administrative post in Kirkby Lonsdale. I had accepted their job offer and moved from Islington to a new home and a new adventure.

Over the next several years, I became a successful hotelier. Now thirty years old, I had been in this role for two years. I was happy and fulfilled in my job – until a phone call completely turned my life around…

… 5.15am on a Sunday morning…

The phone trilled loudly on my bedside table as I fumbled my arm out of the warm duvet cover for the receiver.

'Hello,' I mumbled drowsily.

It was my father, 'Julia...' His voice was frail. *What was wrong!*

'What is it Dad?' I asked, as I knelt on my elbow listening intently for an answer.

'Dad, are you there?'

'Yea... yeah...' his speech was slowly being dragged away from him.

'Dad, what's wrong? I can't hear you very well.' I jolted upright and pushed my hair from my face. Alarm bells rang in my head. I held my breath; something was wrong. My stomach fluttered as if full of butterflies. Negative thoughts rattled my mind.

'It... it... it's your mum,' he stuttered, his last words trailing off as if caught by the wind. 'She's passed away.'

'What!' I shrieked, placing the palm of my hand firmly on the bed. I would never forget those piercing words.

My mum and I had spoken on the phone just last night! How could it be true? It was unbelievable.

The telephone passed from my dad, 'Hello, this is one of the paramedics, we're with your dad right now. I'm sorry to have to tell you that your mum has passed away.' A long moment of silence ensued as those words travelled to my ears again and then into my consciousness.

I scrunched the duvet cover. I could only say, 'Thank you for telling me.' Slowly hanging up the phone, my shoulders slumped as I fought back the tears. *Was this another realm I had woken up into momentarily? Was this a bad dream and I'd wake up soon?*

Disorientated, I wanted desperately to speak to someone. I peeled the duvet back and stumbled out of bed, my legs were shaking. I wasn't sure if they would take my weight. *I must get my telephone book.* My telephone book was in the bedside drawer. I bent over and rummaged through for my book. *Got it.* Flumping down on the side of the bed, my eyes brimmed with tears and fell. I blinked quickly to focus on the numbers. *Stop shaking fingers.* I pushed the numbers on the keypad...

'Hello,' someone said sleepily.

'Hello,' I returned, my voice croaking.

'Is everything ok?'

My throat clogged with grief. I whispered, 'My mum has just died.' I found it hard to breathe out those painful words. I wanted to slam the phone down. My body quaked like a volcano waiting to erupt.

'I'm so sorry,' I heard Jake say tenderly.

I didn't even realise I had phoned him until I heard his voice. It was Rebecca's number I thought I'd dialled.

He cleared his throat, 'Is... is there anything I can do to help? Do you want to talk?'

I heard his words, somewhat disconnected but sincere.

'I just...' I sobbed, 'I just wanted to hear someone's voice.'

Jake was an old college friend who lived a short drive from Kirkby Lonsdale, thirty minutes away, near Ruskin's View. We had remained friends over the last ten years and attended social gatherings of our old university friends. We last met six months ago.

I gripped the phone tightly, but no other words came out. All he could hear were my choked sobs.

'Hey, I'm here for you...' he said as I continued to sob. 'Do you remember the Scripture, "Precious in the sight of the Lord is the death of His saints?"'

I nodded, 'Yes I do.'

'I wish there was something I could do to ease your pain.' He paused.

'I'm so sorry for your loss...'

'Thank you for comforting me with those words... and thank you for being there for me.' Like a pressure cooker I was ready to burst.

'I'll have to go... thanks again,' I sobbed. I hung the receive down. I dropped to the ground in a heap, powerless. Hot tears streamed down my cheeks. I wrapped my arms around my throbbing body. My very being ached. I swayed backward and forward, trying to console myself but finding no solace. My bedraggled hair fell chaotically around my contorted face.

In the darkness and silence of my bedroom, I wailed like a dog who had lost its master. What unbearable sorrow! *Mum, my mum... God, how can this be? My mum... gone... gone.* My heart shattered into fragments of delicate glass that could not be pieced together again. I wanted to scream with all my might. An excruciating pain shot out loudly from within, 'Mumm... no... no... no!'

My eyes, raw from crying, burned as I wept bitterly. 'Help me... God... please,' I howled helplessly as this aching wound engulfed me. Only God could console my crushed heart. Only God could take my hurt away.

+ + +

In the days that followed, although difficult, I spent time at my father's home, with my sisters, Rosie and Keira. I experienced peace, sorrowful as it was. It was God's hand of comfort upon us.

When I returned home after the funeral, people from my local church couldn't have been more supportive. I received many kind cards, visits and phone calls, and offers of home-cooked meals.

God's love, displayed through them, had been so tangible and exactly what I needed at that time. They cared for me as much as my parents would have, and my admiration for them would never waver. I took great comfort and strength in being loved.

Even though I had been overwhelmed with bottomless grief, I sensed that God's love overwhelmed and protected me. His banner over me was of love. I was at peace and assured that one day I would see my mum again in heaven on that glorious day.

+ + +

Jake had been exceedingly kind to me. He had constantly kept in touch by text or phone to let me know he was there for me. I had not realised until then how much of a friend he could be.

I wrote out a Bible scripture Jake had previously texted me. I have it in my Bible today, "He will wipe every tear from their eyes. There will be no more death or mourning or crying or pain, for the old order of things has passed away." This gave me hope that one day, when Jesus returns, there would be no more death or mourning.

Several days later, I finally tried to talk with God, expressing my sorrow and asking Him why He hadn't saved my mum. I sat at the dining room table and tried to read the Bible, but the words blurred. I persisted until the tears subsided. Flipping the pages, I stopped at the Psalms. Psalm 147:3 said, "He heals the broken-hearted and binds up their wounds." *Was this God speaking to me specifically?* Those words comforted me in the days to come.

A week after I arrived back home, Jake called me. He asked whether I would like to take a walk in the countryside with him. I agreed, and he drove to my home in his new yellow jeep. I ambled down the path to meet him, and a warm look of sympathy crossed his face.

We drove to Ashness Bridge in the Lake District. Normally, conversation flowed more easily between us but not that day.

It was a nice day, and I had rolled down the car window halfway. A warm gust of wind quickly blew my hair away from my face. We made small talk on the way. Jake did most of the talking, which I was glad of.

The landscape was stunning. Sunlight blazed like arrows shooting through the trees. The orchestra of birds singing was a wonderful melody to my ears. We parked the jeep and walked along the path, heading towards the bridge before taking the walking trail, which led to some peaceful streams.

I locked my arm through his, not even noticing. I wanted to be close to someone. He didn't object and placed his hand over mine as we continued to meander around a lake. It meant so much to me. Pleased, I watched the shafts of light pouring onto the glistening lake as streams of sunlight bathed the meadow. He asked me if I wanted to talk. I smiled bravely. The pain was still acute.

'I'm still numb from this whole experience,' I said quietly, without looking at him, as a sad smile touched my lips. 'I didn't realise how much losing my mum would affect me.'

'Time is a healer, Julia.'

'That's what they say!' I answered. After a bit of thought, I added, 'I wept aloud until I had no more strength, but I finally found strength in the Lord.'

Jake tenderly whispered, 'Pain is part of living and we have something that only God can give – comfort and strength.'

'Yes... it has been hard going, but... but I sensed God's peace around me even in those early days. I knew God was there with me, as hard as it was.'

I sighed, 'You know, it was Mother's Day, the day my mum died,' my voice quivered slightly, 'and she didn't even have the opportunity to open the card I bought her, or the cards and gifts from my siblings.' Tears stung my eyes as I lowered my eyelids.

Caressing my hand gently, Jake listened attentively without interrupting as we continued to wander around the beautiful lake.

'Mum loved to receive presents and cards on Mother's Day, it was a treat for her.' I started to open my heart. It seemed easy to talk in the open space.

'So many things I wished I had said to her. I treasured her. I treasured her wisdom while I was growing up, even though at times, I must admit, I didn't listen to her,' a small smile formed on my lips. 'I realised later in life that she was right. She was patient in allowing me to find out for myself and never condemned me by saying, "I told you so."'

'She sure sounds like some woman. I met your mum a few times but didn't know her well.'

'Yes, she was some woman, my mum!' We chuckled together, the first time I had laughed since Mum died.

'I knew if I didn't give her a Mother's Day card, she would've been hurt.' I smiled to myself, recalling those pleasant memories. 'She liked to be treated extra special and loved.

'I remember, one year, she was sitting in the armchair in her home with her feet on a foot-stool, with fluffy slippers,' I smiled warmly, 'as she opened her cards that Mother's Day. She took great delight in reading and re-reading every word her children wrote on each card. It was her joy. It always warmed my heart to see her so happy with a broad smile, so refreshing and contagious.'

Jake smiled cheerfully, as we strolled up a steep hill, he grasped my welcoming hand as he led the way. When we reached the top we took in the magnificent view of Skiddaw in the background. What a picturesque backdrop, almost unspoilt. The panorama was breath-taking. Jake took out his phone to capture pictures and brazenly held his camera and took a selfie of both of us. We sat on the grassy slope admiring God's perfect creation.

Jake was dressed in khaki shorts and a white short sleeved shirt.

I smoothed my yellow knee length cotton dress as I tilted my face towards him, and caught a dimple in his chiselled cheek. He turned his head and our eyes locked like magnets. Smiling, I dropped my gaze as a gentle breeze cooled my cheeks.

'When I used to spend weekends with my family, I remember my neighbour saying to me how my mum laughed loudly and so hard that the neighbour laughed too.' Jake's eyes gleamed as he listened to me.

'Her laughter said it all Jake, that's how I'll always picture Mum – with a dazzling smile, full of laughter… I was the last of my siblings to move away from home to London. Mum was hurt that her little baby was leaving… She helped me build my flat into a real home.'

'That's what mums are for, helping their kids out,' chirped in Jake.

'Yes… she did a good job… When she and Dad visited me, she would always wrap her arms around me, full of love and protectiveness, and always held me tightly. I never did say thank you to her properly for enchanting my beautiful home with her mother's touch. Now that I think of this, I am sure she knew in her heart I was thankful because that's the kind of person she was.'

Jake smiled and squeezed my hand, 'I'm sure she did.'

I nodded and continued, 'Even when I was ill Jake, she regularly travelled over two hundred miles to the hospital to see me and make sure I was progressing well. When I was discharged, I needed to convalesce. Mum and Dad came down by car and collected me from Islington, and spoiled me rotten when I arrived at their home.' I smiled brightly, reliving those memories with sheer happiness. 'Those three weeks were one of the most treasured moments in my life. I was much loved.'

Jake patiently listened. I was sure I saw a sparkle in his eyes.

'God gave us mums, and I'm certain that I was born into my family for a reason, not by chance,' I added.

'It's good to reminisce. You have some good, treasured memories of your mum.'

'Hmmm, I do, Jake. I had good times with her that I will always cherish. That is something no one can take away from me. I will miss her greatly, as I will no longer know her warm hand on mine, or see her, or hear her contagious laugh, or watch the room light up when she is around, but I can store precious memories of her in my heart.'

Glancing towards me, Jake said, 'The Bible says in Proverbs chapter 10, "The memories of the righteous are a blessing."'

'I like that. When my mum comes to my mind, I will remember that verse.'

We started to walk leisurely, with my arm still linked with his, as we observed the sunshine filtering through a white speckled butterfly's wings, as it perched on an orange gerbera daisy for a tranquil moment.

Jake remarked, 'How peaceful it is here. The fresh air has given me a raging appetite. Let's go eat. There's a great Asian restaurant up ahead.'

'Sure,' I agreed, even though I didn't have an appetite.

As we were ushered to our seats, the restaurant was busy with tourists. Next to our table was a family with a baby dressed in pink, cooing as her mum cradled her. The sight of new life delighted me, and I wished for a moment I could hold her. Grinning, I enjoyed observing a toddler trying to scramble onto his mum's lap as his father tried to playfully hold him back.

We ordered our meal.

The waitress placed the food before us. Dinner looked and smelt divine. Jake's hungry eyes feasted on the dishes, and he whispered gleefully, 'The food looks scrumptious.' He thanked God for the food and accepted the lunch with gratitude. I ate to keep him company. After all, he had made the effort of driving me this far. A sense of release and peace engulfed me. I was glad to be with him.

We arrived back home late evening. Jake dashed round to the jeep door as I was getting out and held out his hand to reach mine. He walked me to my front door. Laughing, he snapped a few photos to remind us of the memorable day and hugged me. Tears unexpectedly rose to my eyes.

He beamed, 'I've had a good time.'

'Me too. Thank you for taking me. I'm glad I came.'

. +++

Over the next couple of months, I often met him. He was great company, and we could talk for hours. He made me laugh, so much so that at times I was bent over, with my stomach hurting from intense laughter.

Some of Jake's friends had asked him to go out with them, and he wanted me to accompany him. When I saw him, my face glowed, and something pinged inside me. I had made an effort to dress up and noticed him gazing at me in admiration as I happily walked towards his jeep. He had a sparkle and joy in his eye as he caught my smile.

Over the next year, we became more than friends.

One day, we were to meet up at the Old Inn to go horse riding. I was waiting on a nearby bench for him. As he approached, I found myself daydreaming about him and wondering why I hadn't noticed I had fallen in love with him. I found him to be an intelligent man, articulate, positive, confident and handsome. Who would have thought I would fall in love with a guy from the next town whom I had known for years?

+ + +

After an extremely busy season at the hotel, I decided to take three weeks off for a holiday. I was looking forward to some rest.

Bella and Oscar's parents were extremely generous and granted me an additional two days of paid leave to thank me for all the hard work I had put into their business.

At the start of my holiday, Jake asked me to accompany him to a special function at the MacDonald Old England Hotel in Cumbria. A friend of his had organised a get-together for some close friends. Jake was popular, so I wasn't surprised that we would be out for the day.

Arriving at the hotel, I found it was as aesthetic as Jake had said. It was located by Lake Windermere and boasted of a traditional country house charm. I couldn't see Jake's jeep, so I tip-toed in my heels on the gravel path towards the reception. I pushed the door open and casually sauntered in with my clutch bag under my arm. I politely asked the receptionist where the 'Farm Lounge' was located. Jake had requested me to wait there if I arrived before him.

Someone escorted me to a pleasant-looking lounge at the back of the ostentatious hotel. Upon walking into the room, I saw a small bar in front of me. A few people were relaxing around tables, chatting with drinks in their hands, while some were cheerfully playing darts.

I ordered a cold drink and steadily walked towards a vacant round table with three comfy chairs.

Jake had said he would be there at 12.30pm. I became concerned, as it was unlike him to be late. There were no text messages from him and it was 1.00pm already. I called him on his mobile phone. He didn't respond. Perhaps there was no signal on his phone? He had promised he would be here, so I waited patiently.

I wore an off-the-shoulder chiffon evening dress, which Jake had bought me two weeks earlier, specifically for today. I had also worn my hair in a new style because I had wanted to surprise him. It was approaching 1.15pm when he burst in through the door. What a relief! He was looking incredibly dashing, and I stood up to greet him.

His jaw dropped as he spotted me. His eyes fixed on me in admiration. He grinned as his eyes travelled from my head to my feet. He nodded with great approval. My heart fluttered with inexpressible happiness.

'Julia, will you forgive me for my tardiness?'

Smiling back at him, 'I'd forgive you for anything…'

Suddenly, he fell on one knee, took my warm hand into his and whispered in a low tenor, 'Will you marry me?'

Stunned and somewhat bewildered, I gave an exhilarated laugh, 'Yes, I'll marry you.'

As he stood up, I leant forward and wrapped my arms around his strong neck. When I released him from my tender embrace, overjoyed by his proposal, his striking broad smile materialised with his cheeky dimples. His arresting eyes, shone with affection.

I beamed profusely as if the sun was dancing in my heart. Others in the room had seen him kneeling, and their smiling faces shared our joy too. 'Congratulations!' someone shouted, raising their glass in the air towards us as others followed suit.

Jake kissed me quickly, too quickly, and grasped my hand, 'Come on…' he shouted excitedly, as I stretched over and grabbed my clutch.

'I'm coming,' I said joyfully.

He strode with purpose through the lounge, with me following excitedly. We came to a closed door. *I wondered how late we were for his friend's function.* We stood outside for a moment. His eyes shone with enthusiasm, as he gazed at me in adoration.

'I love you more than you'll ever know.'

My smile couldn't have been bigger, 'I love you too…' I thought he was going to kiss me.

He turned towards the door and pushed it open. 'Surprise!' yelled everyone in a chorus as the party poppers went off. All were dressed in wedding attire. My first thought was whose wedding was it, Jake didn't say we were attending a wedding, and then I noticed my father, sisters and the minister of my church. I looked up and a banner read, "Wedding Day of Jake & Julia." Surely not my wedding! It sure was, and the best was yet to come.

After all the wonderful fuss and shock of a surprise marriage, we were chauffeured in style to a car decorated with cans. After we said our goodbyes, Jake drove at the speed of light to our honeymoon destination. Tears of joy rolled down my cheeks as I turned and smiled at him. I knew Mum would be proud of me and would have loved Jake. My heart was effortlessly happy.

The telephone call, over two years ago, which wasn't meant for Jake, certainly had a good outcome!

REFLECTION

- At times, certain circumstances can turn our world around when we least expect it. It may look dire, but good can happen also. "And we know that in all things God works for the good of those who love him, who have been called according to his purpose" (Romans 8:28 NIV).
- Julia grieved and cried out to God, who heard her. When we cry out to God, it may seem He doesn't hear, but He does. He is always there with us, through pain and joy. God was there when Julia experienced grief, and He was there when she experienced joy.
- Julia saw the love of God demonstrated through her church family in her time of need, which gave her immense comfort in her grief.
- Do you have a church family who can support you?
- God delights in us and likes to surprise us. God gave Julia a husband. She didn't search for him. God had already arranged a divine appointment. He is a good God.

WORDS OF WISDOM

Sometimes when we least expect it, God surprises us. In the good and in the bad, He never lets us down. He never leaves us or abandons us.

COLLETTE
Pray Without Ceasing

*"You will seek me and find me
when you seek me with all your heart."
(Jeremiah 29:13 NIV)*

Terror gripped Caleb. Two burly police officers firmly and forcibly clicked cold steel handcuffs around his sprained wrist. His legs wilted as he staggered reluctantly with each step he took towards the muddy police car. Bewildered and disorientated, panic seized his heart.

'God, help me. Please God, help me,' was his deepest cry from within.

Bundled into the car like a bag of useless potatoes, an officer slumped beside him in the back seat without a care in the world, his mouth chewing gum. The officer's cold gaze remained fixed on Caleb, who sat there with eyes etched with despair. The screeching noise and black tyre tracks on the road were the only evidence that they had been there.

+ + +

I was due to be on duty at Exeter Police Station when I received a call asking if I could come in early. The previous duty solicitor was unwell. A man had been arrested and was in a state of shock and had asked to see the duty solicitor.

'Sure, no one I know, I hope?' I replied, humorously.

The officer said, 'A man called Caleb Sterling got arrested for armed robbery.'

I smashed the can of coke I held onto the kitchen table and asked in a tight whisper, 'Who did you say?' my mobile phone stuck to my ear.

'Caleb Sterling. See you soon.'

He hung up before I had the chance to ask another question. I still held on to the can of coke. I shuddered and my stomach sank. Unnerved, I struggled to find composure. I stumbled onto the chair beside the pine kitchen table in disbelief and sat motionless for a moment, letting the news sink in.

A rush of adrenaline spurred me. I changed from casual slacks to a dress and heels and grabbed my coat and car keys. My heart was in my throat as I fumbled the key into the ignition. 'Arrested for armed robbery' played over and over in my head. I inhaled deeply and slowly let out a breath to calm myself. This must be a terrible mistake. It must be...

I spoke aloud, 'Do not be anxious about anything, but in everything, by prayer and petition with thanksgiving, present your requests to God. Philippians 4:6.' I turned to God and started praying.

+ + +

I had met Caleb a year ago while travelling home from visiting my sister, whom I had not seen for months. I stood on the platform at Portsmouth Harbour Rail Station, a wheeled replica Louis Vuitton suitcase in one hand and a matching handbag on my other arm.

The train pulled up and screeched piercingly to a halt. I hurriedly searched for my carriage number and headed to my allocated seat. A pleasant-looking gentleman was seated at a window seat. I stretched to reach up to put my case on the overhead rack. He quickly tried to get up to assist me. Smiling, I dropped my gaze and politely replied,

'I can manage, thank you.'

He eased back into his seat. I took off my jacket, placed it neatly on top of my suitcase, and settled next to him, my back perfectly straight. I retrieved a magazine from my bag and rested the bag between my feet.

We soon engaged in small talk and started chatting to pass the time. His name was Caleb; he was raised in Portchester and lived in Portsmouth. He had received a distressed phone call that morning saying that his mother was desperately sick and he needed to come to Exeter urgently.

He was finishing his coffee when the beverage trolley chinked into the carriage. The uniformed steward had a warm, relaxed smile, and we both ordered a complimentary hot drink.

Caleb also bought a snack. We thanked the steward as he rolled away.

Caleb was jittery. He kept tapping his fingers on the table. His upper eyelids pulled together. My heart went out to him. I wanted to help alleviate his distress.

I so wanted to pray for him, but was nervous as the carriage was full of people. A family played a board game; a young couple seated opposite us were fast asleep, her head resting on his shoulder.

As we continued to talk, I plucked up the courage to ask him if I could pray for his mother. He had said yes without hesitation. I turned slightly to face Caleb, lowered my head, clasped my hands on my lap, and softly prayed.

'God, you know how poorly Caleb's mum Iris is, and I know that Jesus answers prayers. Please touch her body and make her completely well again. In the name of Jesus. Amen.'

I lifted my head, turned it slightly and smiled at Caleb. He returned a faint smile and thanked me for my concern in his deep baritone.

I attempted to lighten the atmosphere by narrating a childhood incident from when I was five years old. I had come into the living room and announced to my parents,

'I can't get the bread out of my nose.'

In all my toddler wisdom, I'd thought that if you could breathe and eat through your mouth, you should be able to do both through your nose too. Caleb grinned. I was glad to have been able to distract him for a while.

As we approached Exeter, I realised that the four-hour journey was already over. I wanted to ensure that all was well with his mother, so I boldly asked Caleb for his phone number. I reassured him that I would continue to pray. He appreciated my thoughtfulness.

Much to everyone's relief, his mother's health improved tremendously. Not long after that, Caleb became a man of God and gave his life to Jesus. Our friendship, which started off as platonic, eventually turned into something more.

The long distant relationship, however, was not practical, and Caleb later secured an advertising job in my hometown, Exeter.

+ + +

As I hurried into the brightly-lit police station, the smell of paint from the freshly-painted white walls tickled my nostrils. The clerk welcomed me at the reception desk as I scanned in and swiftly made my way into the office.

The newly built building included a large custody suite with forty police cells spread over four separate wings. There were additional facilities including access for solicitors and interview rooms.

Once at my desk, in the open-plan office, I promptly turned on my computer, put on my reading glasses, and logged in. I opened the file that was waiting for me. The police report indicated that a video was taken at the scene of the crime.

I rushed to speak to the duty officer. I asked for permission to view the footage as a matter of urgency. My anxiety was palpable, and she decided to allow me to view it. When she loaded the video, I started shaking. There was no doubt in my mind it was Caleb's face. I leant heavily on her desk unable to breathe.

'Are you alright Ms Jarrett?' Her gentle voice calmed me as she rose to lightly grip my shoulder.

Stuttering, I replied, 'Yes.'

I wasn't sure how I would make it back to my desk before seeing Caleb first, but I walked back with my head held high, drawing on inner strength I knew had to come from God.

On my way, an abrupt voice snarled from behind,

'Come now Ms Jarrett.'

Startled, I jumped.

'Your man is guilty as hell…' he quickened his pace to walk beside me, 'guilty of armed robbery.'

I quickly glanced at him, averting my eyes from his steely gaze and hastened my pace as he mumbled,

'You saw the evidence for yourself.'

I blushed. I knew he was telling the truth.

'Video footage showed him at the scene of the crime,' he continued, grinning smugly, 'and he certainly has no alibi... not even you!'

Michael was the only one at the police station who knew that Caleb was my boyfriend. He had asked me out several times. I declined, always saying that I need to give God and myself a good reason for why I'm dating someone. I wanted a man that served Jesus. Michael had never liked my comment.

Caleb was brought to the interview room, where I, as the duty solicitor, would listen to him and give advice. I peeped through the glass window and saw him. He sat with hunched shoulders at the small table, jittery, and tapping his heels. I wanted to hold his hand in mine and tell him everything would be fine. But would it? His agonised face told the story. My heart ached for him as I walked towards the table and settled in a chair opposite him. His wrist was bandaged. His mouth curved into a melancholic smile when he saw me, and his eyes brightened.

'I didn't do it, Collette.' His desperate eyes implored, 'yes, I was there. I must have been framed.' He slouched, his elbow rested on the table as he rubbed his temple.

'Framed by whom?' I inquired.

'I don't even know who he was.'

'Who are you talking about? Who... who is he!? Let's start from the beginning.'

Nodding, he clutched his hands tightly on the table. His knuckles were white. 'I got a phone call around 7.00p.m. asking me to meet him at Dixon Street because someone precious in my life was in danger.' He took a gulp of water from the beaker on the table.

'No number registered on my mobile phone.' A nervous smile broke across his face. 'You know me, Collette, I can't bear the thought of someone I love getting hurt,' he said as a sudden spark flashed in his eyes.

'You didn't recognise his voice?'

'No,' he frowned, 'but... man... it sounded familiar for some reason.'

'Would you be able to recognise the voice again?'

He shook his head. 'I don't know,' he said, dropping his head into both hands.

'I was there because I got the phone call. I... I was pushed hard and fell to the ground. That's how I hurt my wrist,' dropping his gaze at his wrist. 'It all happened in a split second and the next thing I knew, there was a bag beside me... I just can't believe this is happening to me,' as he covered his eyes with both hands.

'Stay with me Caleb... Caleb... Did you see who put it there?'

'No'… inhaling deeply… 'I went to check what was in the bag… it was black, and… before I knew it, police surrounded me… this is so crazy… like a bad dream…' he threw his hands in the air.

I moved closer to him, staring directly into his eyes, 'Was anyone else around as a potential witness?'

'I'm telling you,' his voice rising, 'it all happened so quickly. I didn't see a soul.' He focussed his attention on me, 'Suddenly, I was being roughly handcuffed and a patronising voice was reading me the riot act as I tried to wrap my head around these events.'

'"What's going on?" I yelled. "Robbery," they taunted me. I didn't know what they were talking about!'

'Oh Caleb,' I cried and tenderly stroked his hand, forgetting where I was.

He hung his head in despair, 'I can't believe all this is happening to me.'

I felt powerless and my voice croaked, 'We'll get through this Caleb… somehow.'

He lifted his head and whispered, 'You do believe me, don't you?'

I hesitated. 'I wa… want to believe.'

The loud screeching of the chair startled me. He stood upright, 'What do you mean?! I'm telling you the truth!'

'I saw the video, it's you! What am I to believe?'

The security guard rushed through the door, handcuffed him, and started to lead him away.

Confused, I mumbled, 'Caleb, I don't know what to believe. You did say you needed money.'

He jerked his head and hollered, 'Yes and I told you that God would provide, not a robbery! I didn't do it,' he screamed. His wounded eyes penetrated mine sending shivers down my spine, 'You must believe me, Collette! You must!' He staggered with the guard through the open door.

+ + +

All evidence pointed to Caleb. He had no alibi, was short of money, caught at the scene of the crime, and the video of the store captured someone who looked exactly like him. He was charged with the crime and the preliminary hearing was set four days later.

Bewildered, I stepped out of the police station numbed. I had to listen to my conscience and against all odds, I had to believe Caleb and be there for him.

He had gotten a call from a man, but the number was unknown. I wondered why the voice sounded familiar. He obviously knew the voice, but from where? He was asked to wear his Ralph Lauren jacket to be recognised so the person knew he had one. *Surely, it had to be someone he knew?*

Worry for Caleb had taken its toll on me that day. I didn't know what to do. I drove home after work in a daze and shut the door quietly behind me. I leant against it momentarily as the warmth of the room welcomed me. I slid down where I stood, as my strength evaporated from me.

Somehow, I crawled to the couch, leaving my handbag and keys where they fell. Molly, my Burmese cat, ran down the stairs as I held on to the arm of the couch and sobbed, 'Lord, you know the truth. I want to believe Caleb but there is no evidence for what he is saying. All the evidence shows that he is guilty.' I slumped to the ground. My head bowed in reverence as burning tears streaked down my cheeks and silently sunk into the carpet. 'Show me the truth… please God, show me the truth.' I kept repeating softly as my body trembled with sobs.

Before I snuggled into my warm duvet, I called the pastor of my church, Pastor Williams, and told him what had happened. He was as stunned as I had been. He prayed over the phone with me,

"Lord, if the man who had called Caleb exists, convince that person to give himself up."

'Collette, remember whatever happens, God's love for Caleb is a love that is steadfast and unshakable. It's a love that endures forever,' he advised, 'When you have God on your side, you can make it. And don't forget to pray without ceasing.'

Before I fell asleep, I prayed, prayed, and prayed some more. What else could I do?

+ + +

The next morning, I could hear the rain pelting against the windowpanes. I woke to a loud pounding at the door. Drowsy from sleep, I smothered a yawn and stretched my arm out from under the duvet to retrieve my mobile from the bedside table. I squinted towards it and quickly jumped out of bed and stepped onto the cold floor. I peeked out the window. It was the neighbourhood postman. I wasn't expecting a parcel. Grabbing my furry dressing gown, I rushed downstairs.

My sister's address was on the return label. What a pleasant surprise, it must be a belated birthday present. As I opened it, my eyes widened. The words written on the scenic beach plaque were "Trust him." "Trust him", as if my sister knew exactly what I was going through.

With a sigh of relief, I nestled down on the floor before the fireplace in my new chic home and watched the red and yellow flames in the imitation fire swirl as it warmed the air. Molly waltzed in purring for attention and curled up satisfied on my lap. She quietly watched the flames as I stroked her tenderly. I opened my Bible, which was resting on the ceramic tiles, and began to read Genesis 42:21, 'Then they said to one another, "Truly we are guilty concerning our brother, because we saw the distress of his soul when he pleaded with us, yet we would not listen; therefore, this distress has come upon us."'

Joseph's eleven brothers were jealous of him and later sold him into slavery. They saw the distress in their brother's eyes. I had also seen the distress in Caleb's pleading eyes. I must help Caleb with God's help, but how?

I bowed my head and clasped my hands, 'Lord, show me what to do, please show me what to do.' I hadn't yet told his mother of this misery because of the pain I knew it would cause her. I had to do something immediately.

Since it was the weekend, I called Iris, Caleb's mum, and informed her I'd be stopping by to see her. I didn't explain the reason, I needed to break the news to her face to face.

I had breakfast, although it was forced, as I needed my strength, and set out for the three-hour drive to visit her. It was always disheartening to look at the faded wallpaper on every wall in the house and listen to the noisy banging from the radiator. The noise was especially unwelcome today when I needed to have a serious conversation.

Iris wanted the house to remain the same as when her beloved husband was alive. She had fond memories that she didn't want to erase. She made up for it with her warm smile and elegant charm. She was always pleased to see me.

Iris was frail, but I needed to know if she could help Caleb in any way. I broke the news gently to her. She wasn't as shocked as I had expected. She remained thoughtful and calm, which surprised me. I couldn't understand until she started to tell the story of Caleb's past.

'Collette, I have something to tell you.'

'Oh,' I said frowning wondering what it could be.

'Caleb had been in trouble when he was younger. He had had a nervous breakdown and lost his memory. His mind was a complete blank.' My stomach twisted hearing those disturbing words. That would explain the mystery of what had happened.

'But... what caused his nervous breakdown?' I asked puzzled.

She began to tell me the full story.

Afterwards, Iris was, of course, concerned about Caleb but we had caught up, and as usual she prayed before I left. We were both saddened that Caleb was in custody but relieved that he was still alive. We had faith in God.

In a fleeting moment, it all made sense. I had seen the video for myself. It was Caleb in the store, there was no question in my mind. Yet my gut feeling said otherwise. *What was wrong?* I thought I had known everything there was to know about Caleb. But now that I had learnt this disturbing news from his mum, it changed everything. I was agitated. All the evidence was stacked high against him.

Uneasy, I settled myself in the car, ready for my drive home and paused to pray, 'Father God, I don't know what to believe. Caleb has never lied to me and yet it looks as if he is guilty of a terrible crime. If... if he is innocent, you have the power to change hearts, lives, and circumstances. Whoever framed him, may they be convicted of what they have committed and have no peace. I want to know the truth. You are the truth. Tell me the truth. Is Caleb innocent or guilty? I ask this in Jesus' name. Amen.'

By the time I left, it was 6.00pm and darkness had crept in slowly. My long journey home wasn't lonely as I knew that Jesus was with me.

+ + +

On Monday, after reading my emails at work, I visited Caleb.

In a matter of days, the stress had taken a toll on his body. He slouched at the table, thinner than before. He had dark circles beneath his eyes, which were starting to look like bruises.

'Caleb, how are you doing?' *What else could I ask?* We sat around the wooden table in the interview room.

'Not great.' He admitted in a low voice, drumming his fingers on the table. 'I've been finding it hard to pray and struggling to make sense of why this is happening to me.'

His voice was distressed. He swept his greasy raven hair backwards.

Keeping my composure wasn't easy. I placed my clasped hands on the table to keep calm. I wanted to embrace him. My aching heart yearned for him. But I had to be strong. 'Have you any idea, any inkling why someone would want to do this to you?'

'None at all, I'm as lost as you.' A tear fell from his sad eyes, his cheeks inflamed. There was so much pressure on him.

'I went to see your mum yesterday. I'm sorry, but I needed to know how I could help.' I lowered my eyes and mumbled, 'She said you had a nervous breakdown when you were younger?'

Caleb's nostrils flared. 'A nervous breakdown,' he yelled. 'I've never had a nervous breakdown, Collette.'

He immediately apologised for the sudden outburst. This was the first time I had seen Caleb in this state. What else should I have expected? He was facing a long prison sentence.

My eyes penetrated his restless ones darting back and forth. Trying to make sense of things, I gently said, 'Your mum said you would forget things, and perhaps you can't remember having a nervous breakdown because you don't want to remember?'

He sulked, 'Did she say what caused the breakdown?' His eyes searched for an answer.

'Yes, she explained it was over a girl that you were in love with.'

He shook his head, 'Yes, Sally. I was in love with her a long time ago, long before I met you. Remember I told you about "Bon Bon"?'

'Yes?' I replied inquisitively.

'Bon Bon is Sally, it was her nickname.'

'What a funny name.'

'Yes, it is. It did hurt when it was over, but I didn't have a nervous breakdown. Why would Mum say such a thing?'

'I don't know,' I whispered, deep in thought.

His mother said he wouldn't remember, and he certainly didn't. His mother was known to be trustworthy and faithful — a pillar when you needed support.

We chatted for a few more minutes before I left.

Exhausted, I took an extended lunch break with some accrued overtime. I had to go to the scene of the crime. *Why hadn't I before?* I drove the twenty arduous miles to the scene.

The exclusive boutique was in a quiet suburban area. It was located on a sharp bend. Caleb was found further down the road. I didn't know what I would find there, arriving in the middle of the day. Grey clouds were beginning to form. I parked the car in the store's car park and walked the rest of the way. The wind howled as I wrapped my long cashmere coat tightly around my slender waist. A squall hit me without warning, spinning a heap of dried leaves on the ground like a tornado near my feet.

I trudged against the wind towards the glamorous shop and pushed the revolving door. A gust of warm air welcomed me in.

Once inside, I straightened my hair and stood tall. I observed, with awe, the dazzling colour coordination of dresses and footwear, tops and trousers, lingerie and sleepwear. It truly was a high-end store. The bright lights created a warm and homey atmosphere. Lights bounced off the imitation diamond studded dresses on the mannequins, creating a sensational display.

The extravagant store was everything I had heard it to be since its refurbishment. Sales assistants chatted happily with customers or busied themselves tidying the racks to show the clothes at their best.

As I strolled towards the beauty counter, I noticed how smartly dressed the staff were. They wore tailored navy-blue pin-striped dresses and had exquisite makeup and hairdos. One of the courteous and friendly staff asked if I needed any assistance. I said, 'No thank you, I'm just browsing.' I didn't know what I was browsing for. I glanced at the many cash tills and forced myself to picture the scene. How frightened the staff must have been.

The shop assistant who spoke to me earlier was at a counter, waiting for customers. I walked over and browsed the perfumes. 'What perfume would you recommend?' I asked politely.

She was happy to help, 'I personally like the floral scents.' She busied herself showing me the various new perfumes they had from France. I gently sniffed the first perfume. What a delicate fragrance. It was gorgeous.

I gathered my courage and asked, lifting another scent to my nose as I spoke, 'I heard there was an incident in the store a few days ago?'

'Oh! Yes,' she gasped, placing her hand on her chest. 'It was horrible.' She shook her head and stared at me. 'I was in the shop that day.'

'You were?' I said astonished. 'It must have been frightening.'

'It was.' She placed more expensive perfumes on the counter for me to sample.

'One moment the man was as friendly as can be, and then he started demanding money with a gun in his hand.'

'Oh my!' I responded, spraying the perfume on my wrist, and taking in the fragrance, forgetting the seriousness of the crime for which Caleb would receive a harsh sentence if found guilty.

She smiled when she saw my eyes sparkle as I delighted in the fragrance of the perfume.

'Yes, it was something you wouldn't want to relive,' she fluttered her eyelids, 'he was incredibly nervous as if he didn't want to be doing it.' She busied herself with placing the tester perfumes back in place. 'Times are hard for many people.'

'I guess so.' I replied. 'I think I'll buy the Verset "It's Done", please.'

'Good choice madam, I have some myself,' she said with a cheery smile as she wrapped the scent neatly into a shiny new box.

I said a friendly goodbye and sauntered out of the shop, happy with my purchase.

My happiness soon evaporated as I returned to reality. I turned down the bend, recalling the main reason I had taken time to be here. I headed straight down the street where Caleb had been arrested.

The wind had died down, but the street was deserted; there didn't seem to be anyone around. Each footstep I took echoed in my ear. It was a little eerie.

I noticed a secluded alleyway. Odd that Caleb didn't say anything about an alleyway. He said he was pushed hard and fell. I wondered if someone came out of the alley and then returned the same way.

Why would they frame Caleb and for what purpose? It didn't make sense. What kind of enemies did he have?

Determined, I strutted down the narrow, cobbled alleyway in my flat shoes, black handbag over my shoulder, and a small bag of perfume in the other hand searching for anything that could help Caleb. A cat startled by my presence, scurried away banging against a dustbin and hissing as it went.

The alley led to a long wooden fence, some of which was dilapidated. It lined the backyards of some houses. Each separate stretch of the fence had a garden gate. Whose doors were these? On the opposite side of the alley was a high red mellow brick wall with numerous cracks. I promptly took a video of all the doors, but the fence was too high to peep over. Then I swiftly shuffled out of the alleyway before someone noticed me snooping around. If the person came from the alley, he or she must have come from one of those doors. Which one?

Threatening clouds darkened and a storm began to brew. I quickened my steps to the car and carefully drove home.

+ + +

I studied the video on my phone. There were seven back doors in the alleyway. I straight away decided to knock on each front door and see if someone heard or even saw anything that might help Caleb.

The following day, before I arrived at work in the afternoon, I visited those seven houses and knocked on each front door. At door number five, I was met with a well-dressed young woman adorned with vintage makeup. She looked familiar, but I couldn't figure out where I had seen her before. She recognised me from somewhere too and was hesitant. I asked her if she heard or knew anything about the incident.

'I don't know anything… sorry,' she said hastily, and shut the door on me. I left, puzzled. Where had I seen her before? Was there a connection?

While working that afternoon, I had an opportunity to see Caleb and tell him about the young lady, but he also didn't recognise her description. Caleb was brighter today, and a warmth came over my heart.

Beyond reasonable doubt, all evidence pointed to Caleb. There were still no leads. Yet, I believed he was innocent.

After work, on my way home, I prayed, 'God help me, please. I need some wisdom as to what to do.' I suddenly had an intense feeling that I should return to the crime scene. Something did not add up. I knew that girl from number five but how? What was it that caught my eye from the door? Yes! The jacket! It was on the back of a chair and looked remarkably similar to the one Caleb was instructed to wear that day. I knew he wore that jacket often. Was it a coincidence?

Later that evening, Iris phoned me asking how I was. I told her about the jacket and that I had no proof it was connected to Caleb's crime. Iris spoke gently to me, asking me to take care of myself as she knew I would do everything to help Caleb. But her next words left me aghast.

'Collette, you're prying too much into stuff that you know nothing about. I'm his mother. I know him better than you. Let the police take care of this.'

Angry and profoundly upset, I ended the conversation trying to be as pleasant as I could. How could she say such things?

Like a boxer in a ring thrashing his opponent, I grabbed a cushion with both hands, buried my nails into it, and bashed it against the chair repeatedly with every ounce of strength I had. Weary and exhausted, I finally collapsed, still clinging to the cushion and crying like an infant. Pastor Williams' words came to mind as I huddled on the floor "Pray without ceasing." I closed my eyes tightly and muttered desperately, 'God, help me... please... and help Caleb.'

+ + +

Caleb had been in custody for four weeks already. After we had the preliminary hearing, a date was set for his trial.

The day of his trial came, and still, no new evidence.

A hushed silence filled the courtroom. The sentence was being read. Caleb was sentenced to five years in prison. Hot tears scalded my face. My body failed me, collapsing on itself. Ruth, who had attended court with Pastor Williams, rushed to my side to help me. Together, we stumbled out of the court in total disbelief. Ruth held me, putting her loving, supportive arm around my waist as I stumbled out of court.

'God, why him? Why did this happen?' I wailed. I couldn't understand. 'We prayed and prayed and...'

There was no answer from God or from Ruth. It shook my faith. I had expected a miracle to happen. My heart ached like a branch severed from a tree.

Several days after the sentence, Pastor Williams and Ruth came to my home for a visit. They were kind and comforting. They said that God's thoughts are not our thoughts, neither are His ways our ways, and we may not be able to understand why God sometimes allows things to happen, but we can still choose to trust in His love. It was hard for me to comprehend what they were saying. I knew in my heart that God's comfort can come to us through the support of others, through words of reassurance, and hope in the Bible. I felt a little encouraged.

Oftentimes I would reflect on the words that Pastor Williams gave me right at the beginning: "Pray without ceasing." As hard as it was — and believe me, there were times I wanted to give up and admit defeat — I kept praying even though Caleb was already in prison.

The year passed quickly, and I kept praying. My church continued to pray monthly for Caleb. They never stopped. This was a great comfort to me. He had now been in prison for over a year without any sign of freedom.

+ + +

One day, to my surprise, I spotted a well-dressed lady in the mall; it was the woman from number five. She hadn't noticed me. I followed her discreetly. She spoke to a man, but I couldn't see his face. They disappeared amongst the crowd of shoppers. I thought it was strange that I should see her again after all this time.

Later in the day, I received a phone call requesting me to attend the police station urgently. I wasn't due at work that day and became curious.

I parked the car and quickened my steps to the sliding doors. Sally escorted me to a room. As I entered, I was taken aback. In front of me was the well-dressed young lady and Caleb, in a stylish suit. The lady held herself rigidly, tension etched on her face, and Caleb was fidgeting in a way I'd never seen before. He wouldn't meet my eyes. What was going on? Why was Caleb here and not in prison? As I stood there confused, I was told the story...

'Thirty-six years ago, Iris... Mum, was pregnant. She wasn't aware that she was carrying twins until late in her pregnancy. My dad worked abroad in Australia; he didn't know about the twins. Times were hard. He was still abroad when the babies were born. At home, Iris had already planned to sell one of the babies to a desperate mother who had lost her baby years before. So, everyone was happy. Dad had no idea she had given birth to twin boys. I was the other identical twin, I am Ric.'

I gasped in disbelief.

'I found out I was adopted when my adoptive mother broke the news to me before she died. I was devastated. After years of searching, I eventually found out who Iris was and where she lived. I'm ashamed to say that I had threatened to tell her secret, as well as harm her and Caleb if she didn't cooperate with me.

'My adopted family was poor but loving. I felt betrayed thinking Caleb had it all while I had nothing. I had planned the robbery meticulously for the past year so I could pin the blame on Caleb as revenge for what I had missed.

'This is my wife, Jessica. She had been the one who pushed Caleb to the ground and sped back through the alleyway to our home. Jessica had been attending the same church Caleb and you attend, in disguise. We both had been following Caleb secretly for months to observe his movements and attire.

'Throughout this year, I have been tormented, feeling I should give myself up, but I feared the penalty. I can no longer take the torment — the sleepless nights, the need to constantly look over my shoulder — no peace, no life for me but torture. I couldn't take it anymore so I've finally surrendered.'

Ric flicked his shame-filled eyes up and catches mine as I stared at him with sadness.

+ + +

Ric received a prison sentence of seven years and Jessica a community service sentence. I later found out that Iris had lied about Caleb having a nervous breakdown to protect Caleb. It must have gone against everything she believed. She loved her son.

Caleb was freed. Free indeed. We could not express our gratitude and be thankful enough to God for setting him free. Justice was done. It was a hard road. But I am grateful that I did not give up on praying for Caleb and forever indebted to the good church that stood by me and Caleb.

+ + +

Three months later, on a bright and windy day, the luscious green branches of the sturdy sycamore tree swayed in the delightful summer breeze, giving off a pleasant scent like freshly pressed laundry. The cheery breeze rustled through the leaves with unseen fingers.

Squinting in the midday sunshine, I chased my summer hat, bare-footed, as it tumbled in the wind towards the meadow. I watched it roll down the slope, away from me.

Earlier, Caleb and I had devoured our picnic lunch. I had prepared some homemade chickpea salad sandwiches and avocado summer rolls, which we followed up with cold, refreshing passion fruit juice. We had been clearing up the plates when a sudden gust of wind blew off my straw hat as Caleb struggled to hold down the chequered blanket from taking flight.

I scooped and caught the hat awkwardly without tripping down the hill and placed it firmly on my head. As I leisurely meandered back up the hill, I saw that Caleb was happily lounging with his back against the trunk of a shaded tree, hands behind his head, without a care in the world.

Lowering myself to the ground, I cuddled up beside him. I pondered, 'It's hard to believe I am forty-four years old now, and my daughter, Emily, a feisty thirteen-year-old.'

'It's hard to believe I am thirty-seven years old, and every day I enjoy my freedom!'

We giggled like teenagers.

'Caleb, how amazing to be under this old sycamore tree that has been standing since before we were even born. How wonderful to forget all the cares of the world in this moment.'

I relaxed against his chest. My head nestled against his broad shoulders as I stretched my lanky legs out and finally rested with my legs crossed. His arms wrapped around my waist as I snuggled closer to him.

'You know I love Emily, don't you, Collette?' His warm breath whispered against my ear. 'I love her as if she was my own child.'

'I know you do.'

I shifted my position slightly, beaming with approval as I looked deep into his eyes. I lingered there for a moment and said sombrely,

'We've been through a lot. It makes one appreciate how important and treasured life is.'

'Yes, it does.' Raising an eyebrow, he brushed his cheek against mine, breathing in my perfume.

He then kissed my cheek. I beamed.

He kissed my eyelids and tipped up my chin. Tenderness washed over my heart, and I lifted my face to meet his lips and kissed him longingly.

He held me tighter and placed his chin on my shoulder.

'We trust God and must use our time wisely. I want to do that. I want to share the rest of my life with you, Collette. Will you be my wife?', he whispered.

Bubbling with enthusiasm, I swivelled around and knelt beside him. I wrapped my arms around his neck and drew his head down till our lips touched, giving him my answer.

'I love you, Caleb. I've loved you ever since I met you on the train.'

We broke apart and our gazes locked. The joy shining in his eyes lifted my heart. As my hand slid to the back of his neck, my lips were an inch away from his sweet smile.

I promised, 'I will always love you,' and drew him into another embrace.

Thrilled with this happy turn of events and thankful to God that Caleb still loved Jesus, my heart was full to bursting for answered prayers. It was so easy to give up when I didn't see any evidence of my prayers being heard. But God was working behind the scenes all the time.

+ + +

A year later, in my local church, Caleb and I ambled arm-in-arm down the flower-decked aisle. I wore the dress my mother had worn at her wedding, embellished with rare antique lace.

One of the guests on the groom's side wondered where we had met and asked her great-granddaughter sitting beside her.

'Gran, they met on a train. Not only that, but she also took the plunge and asked him for his number!'

The old lady asked with awe, 'She did?' A twinkle shone in her eyes as she gleefully chuckled softly to herself. 'There's hope for me then!'

The great-granddaughter's jaw dropped as she turned her head to gawk at her ninety-seven-year-old Gran in amazement!

REFLECTION

- Collette believed in the impossible and continued to pray; she prayed without ceasing.
- Collette prayed, expecting Caleb to be set free. When it didn't happen, she was devastated. Have you prayed for something that didn't turn out as you expected? Did you see God differently after that?
- Collette prayed even after Caleb was convicted of a crime.
- Caleb, even though he went through a distressing time, still had faith in God. When we go through a testing time, do we still hold on to God's anchor?
- Although it is not mentioned, do you think Caleb forgave his mother, brother, and sister-in-law for what they did to him?
- Iris went against her beliefs and lied about her son. She was threatened with harm to herself and Caleb. What would you have done in her situation?
- Have you ever been falsely accused?

WORDS OF WISDOM

Sometimes we want to give up on praying for someone or something. We can easily give up when we don't see any results. When we are praying in line with God's word, continue to pray without ceasing. You never know: that prayer might be answered just when you want to give up!

We may even have been falsely accused and couldn't be vindicated despite all our efforts. Be assured God knows the truth. He is our vindicator.

WHAT A FRIEND WE HAVE IN JESUS

What a Friend we have in Jesus,
All our sins and griefs to bear!
What a privilege to carry
Everything to God in prayer!
O what peace we often forfeit,
O what needless pain we bear,
All because we do not carry
Everything to God in prayer!

Have we trials and temptations?
Is there trouble anywhere?
We should never be discouraged,
Take it to the Lord in prayer.
Can we find a friend so faithful
Who will all our sorrows share?
Jesus knows our every weakness,
Take it to the Lord in prayer.

Are we weak and heavy-laden,
Cumbered with a load of care?
Precious Saviour, still our refuge--
Take it to the Lord in prayer;
Do thy friends despise, forsake thee?
Take it to the Lord in prayer;
In His arms He'll take and shield thee,
Thou wilt find a solace there.

Written by Joseph M Scriven (1819-86)

AMBER
The Wedding Gown

"That is why a man leaves his father and mother and is united to his wife, and they become one flesh."
(Genesis 2:24 NIV)

Great enthusiasm filled my merry heart on this radiant, beautiful morning. My wedding day was finally here! Despite being a fitness fanatic, there would be no brisk walk in the neighbourhood park that morning, no matter how much I desired it.

The cloudless sky on that glorious summer day announced the wedding of the perfect couple, Amber and Jeremy.

It was 9.00am at my childhood family home. The sun was glowing brightly, preparing for this joyous occasion. Birds whistled happily outside, their songs carried on the heavenly aroma of roses, drifting in through the open French windows of my bedroom.

I was eternally grateful to God for answering my prayers and making my dreams a reality.

The cool shower ran over my tumbling mass of auburn hair. I was glad this was my last day as a singleton. Alice, a qualified cosmetologist and friend of the family, would be arriving at 9.15am to style my luscious hair and manicure my nails.

My beautiful, silk gown with a voluminous skirt would create an enchanting effect when I walked down the aisle. The pure white gown was perfect for me. The skirt had been delicately decorated with hand-placed pearl beads and a silk belt to accentuate my straight figure.

Everything was arranged neatly in the spare bedroom. I loved to look at the gown so I laid it out neatly across the Georgian bed alongside my elbow-length, two-tier, white veil. These were accompanied by the elaborate bridal hair vine and the glistening tiara. Being a professional seamstress, Jenny, my sister, had helped me choose the gown and added some alterations. She had also designed a few simple yet elegant and classy dresses for my honeymoon.

At fifty-six years of age, I had never been married or even kissed before. Hard to believe but it's true.

Kissing was a big temptation for Jeremy and me. We had agreed not to kiss each other, not even on the cheek (Jeremy was certainly a gentleman and kissed me on my hand). We wanted to wait until our wedding day, as we felt kissing would easily escalate into sexual intimacy for us. Jeremy wanted to wait until we were man and wife to honour God and to honour me. I had great respect for him. It felt special that he wanted to make a permanent commitment to me first.

A sixty-two-year-old man, with laughing eyes, Jeremy would no longer be a widower after 3.00pm today!

We met at a Bible seminar titled 'Called to be Single' at Spring Harvest, a well-known Christian conference event. It was apparent that we were not called to remain single! After a short engagement, 16 June was set as the date for our wedding.

Reaching for the conditioner, I was distracted for a moment as the clatter of cutlery and crockery downstairs signalled the serving of breakfast. Certainly, a happy sound to me! My dad, step-mum Florence, baby sister Jenny (well, baby to me at twenty-five years younger!), Jenny's husband Rob, and Carter, their four-year-old son, were all together at the family breakfast table.

When my parents were married, people gossiped because Mum was twenty-one years older than my dad. Gossipers said the marriage would not last. But last it did. Mum was forty-four when I came into the world, two years after my brother, Jonnie. I wish she was still with us to enjoy this day.

Above the noise of the shower, I heard a loud knocking on the bedroom door. 'Who is it?' I called...

'It's me, Jenny.'

I shouted from the bathroom, 'Come in.' Drying myself gently, I slipped swiftly into my cool dressing-gown.

'Breakfast is ready,' yelled Jenny through the closed bathroom door, 'I didn't want you to miss out.'

I didn't want breakfast, but she persuaded me and thrust a silver breakfast tray onto the small, square table beside my petite armchair. Two slices of toast with marmalade, a boiled egg and a glass of orange juice.

+ + +

Jenny and I were close. A few weeks earlier, we had a great time gathering outfits and accessories for my honeymoon in Santorini, an idyllic Greek island. Window shopping was always fun for us sisters and that day had been no different. We both sported identical smiles all day long. We laughed and shopped till we were exhausted. As we linked our arms together, we strolled, giggling like schoolgirls, enjoying the moment and cherishing the bond we shared. Our hearts aflutter for the future, we began to reminisce.

'Remember the first day Jeremy came to meet Dad and the family?' I gaily recalled.

'Yeah, he was nervous – sweating like crazy, the poor thing! And when he pulled his handkerchief out, he fumbled and dropped...'

We burst into hysterics.

'He… he… dropped a pink dummy! And that look on Dad's face… do you think he thought you were pregnant?! And Jeremy's over-enthusiastic grab could have definitely snapped the dummy in two,' Jenny trilled, 'when he scrambled to retrieve it, and it just bounced away.'

Laughter erupted again. 'He didn't know where to look!' I roared. 'He went as red as a radish. Did you see his face?' Another burst of hysterical laughter ensued.

When we eventually calmed down again, I sighed sweetly and remarked, 'He did explain it was his granddaughter's, not his.' Smiling heartily, 'I was so happy. And he relaxed soon enough when he realised how warm and loving our family is.'

'Yeah, he sure did,' resounded Jenny.

+ + +

'Alice is here, by the way,' Jenny announced happily, interrupting my reverie.

Comfortably seated on the dresser stool with my back against the wall, I dried my hair with the towel.

On cue, Alice walked in with a smile on her face. She drank in the beauty of the large, charming room with a deep breath. 'So good to see you again, Amber.' She strolled towards the bare dressing table beside my chair and my breakfast, and heaved her heavy bag down before turning to embraced me.

'Alice, hi – good to see you too. Beautiful day, isn't it?' I replied happily.

'Sure is. I'm so excited for you Amber… your day is finally here,' she said as she took the towel gently from me. 'I'm here now, so I'll be looking after you. Once I've sorted your hair, I'll do your toes and nails. Are we still having the natural nude colour?'

'Yes, definitely, I think it would complement my skin tone.'

+ + +

My wedding day had an unexpected dilemma I didn't know the whole story until Jenny told me…

'Dad's study door was usually locked. In the hubbub, he must have left it open that day – and what could be more inviting to my mischievous four-year-old than an open door to Grandad's mysterious study?

Carter told me he was alone in the corridor. With no one watching, he tiptoed into the study. He told me he climbed onto the office chair. He saw the colourful indelible marker pens lying on the desk and decided to scribble on the documents.

Grandad's architectural work was laid out on the floor. He tried decorating the drawings with limited success.

When he finished he went into the spare bedroom, where he liked to play with the teddies… but of course the teddies and toys were packed away, and there before him was your wedding gown on the bed.

I heard him singing and went to investigate. I was frozen with shock and my feet felt as if they were glued to the carpet as I saw the gown and smelled the odour of the permanent markers. Carter was happily drawing away on the bodice of your dress. I asked him what was he doing and he rubbed his hands gleefully and beamed at me, and then he said,

"I did finish my picture Mummy. Do you like Auntie Amber's colouring?"

I struggled to stop myself from raising my voice at him. Your wedding gown was completely ruined. I didn't know what to do. I grabbed Carter in my arms and rushed him downstairs to Mum.

Mum read the troubled look in my eyes. I asked her to make sure that Carter stayed with her for the rest of the morning as I had urgent work to do. I didn't give Mum any time to respond as I fled. Poor Mum, she was left cuddling my fidgety young rogue and trying to stop him wiggling into his next adventure as she wondered what was going on.

I went back to the bedroom and inspected the gown. There were tears in my eyes – I was trying not to panic.

I didn't know how I would explain this to you Amber, one of the happiest days of your life and this had happened. The ink would not come out in the wash. How could I repair the damage? It was 9.30am, and there wasn't much time before the wedding at 3.00pm. I tried to think and I prayed a desperate prayer to God for help, or wisdom, or anything.

Concealing my concerns, I pretended to be cheerful when I told you I was popping out and would be back shortly. You were in the armchair, not a care in the world chatting to Alice as your toenails were being shaped and painted.

I went to a charity shop where I knew the mannequins in the window always had appealing clothes and where I knew they sold wedding dresses. I found two white silk gowns; to my relief one of the gowns was virtually identical to the gown you had, only a size larger. It was in impeccable condition. The bodice was so amazing I felt breathless with excitement. As I looked I realised the gown was more gorgeous than yours.

I thanked God I had found an exquisite gown and for such a bargain. I purchased it, rushed to the car, and drove like a crazed woman through the town. My heart was galloping like a horse on a racetrack, bolting to reach the finish line. I prayed fervently all the way home that Mum still had her sewing machine.

When I got back and explained to Mum what had happened, I was thankful to learn the sewing machine was in the house. I went in the back room downstairs so you wouldn't hear the noise of the machine being used.

Dressmaking is second nature to me, as you know. As I studied the dress it seemed more spectacular than at first glance. In all my days as a seamstress, never had I seen a gown so remarkably stunning, Amber. I carefully removed the front bodice wondering how I would secretly collect your gown without anyone noticing. Fortunately, a quick scan on everyone's locations found you were all well occupied, and I slipped in and out of the spare bedroom without being noticed.

I removed the stained front bodice of your gown and remarkably achieved a perfect replacement. Obviously I knew your size, so I stitched up the extra material to ensure that it fitted just as perfectly. I design a lot of clothes, but wedding gowns are a new area for me. Looking back, I'm impressed I managed to get so proficient so quickly.

It was 1.30pm when I finished working. I carefully took the gown back upstairs and placed it on a hanger. Phew – what a relief!'

+ + +

When Jenny finished telling the story, she said, 'I'm sure your heart was in your throat Amber?'

'It was.' I rushed into the spare bedroom, and saw the gown hanging on the wardrobe. My fears were banished, and my face radiant. The gown was more exquisite than the original. It was resplendent.

Excitedly, I tried it on. Perfection! It seemed the gown was made in heaven purely for me. God, evidently, was looking after me. He loves me so much.

+ + +

My beautiful long tresses fell tenderly behind my smooth shoulders in a French pleat. My braid was charmingly decorated by the elaborate hair vine, and it looked gorgeous against the silk gown. It beautifully complimented my earrings and the intricate beading on my gown.

Alice secured my tiara to the front of my neatly combed hair and fixed the veil in place.

My step-mum entered the bedroom, leaving Carter with his dad. Great admiration filled her as words of happiness quivered out of her tiny lips. 'You look… breath-taking.' A warm smile then filled her joyful face as she reminisced about her own wedding day, thirty-four years earlier.

How Jenny managed to get ready and prepare Carter as a page boy in time, I don't know. Somehow, there they were at my bedroom door dressed in wedding day finery. Carter hadn't even had time to pull off his clip-on bow-tie yet.

As sisters we stopped for a moment, clasped our warm hands together reassuringly, joined hands with my step-mum and Alice, and prayed a thankful prayer to God. 'Father God, thank you for this beautiful day. May it be a day to honour you as Jeremy and Amber stand before you as man and wife. Thank you that their meeting was not by chance but a gift from you. We give you this day. In Jesus' name. Amen.'

'Amen,' we all heartily chimed, even young Carter, with a beautiful grin.

Though often seen as a weary-faced man, my dad was overwhelmed by a mixture of sheer delight and love. He beamed with admiration as he witnessed me - in his eyes, his beautiful daughter – walk elegantly down the red-carpeted staircase. Like an artist painting by chance and skill, an unexpected masterpiece, he gasped at me. I held my gown, lifted ever so slightly, as I carefully took each step down the spiral staircase. My voluminous skirt trailed majestically behind me. The sleeveless silhouette bodice was perfect for me.

Meeting in the hallway below, Dad moved slowly towards me with outstretched arms as I glided down the last step, with my head lifted high, I walked like royalty towards him. For a brief moment, our hands met in a warm embrace. I said nothing. He said nothing. My caring touch and a single tear on Dad's face said it all. Peace settled in our hearts.

'You look magnificent,' my admiring dad eventually said, 'If your mother could see this day, she would be as proud of you as I am.' His wrinkled eyes were clouded with more warm tears.

As we embraced, our cheeks met and I knew Dad hoped that time would stand still a little while to enable him to savour that moment. His mind was flooded with good memories of my mum, a wife and a mother who had brought great joy and love.

+ + +

Jeremy would be at the church now and likely anxious as I was late for my own wedding!

Blissful, I gracefully step out of the bronze Rolls Royce, lifted by the firm hand of my proud dad.

The church bells rang melodically to Handel's Messiah, and 'Hallelujah' filled the air with joy and happiness. Fragrant bouquet in hand, I smiled effervescently at the cameras snapping away at my every turn, making me feel like a celebrity as we headed towards the church doors.

The procession began with the flower girl, one of Jeremy's granddaughters. As we entered the church, the 'Wedding March' started to play. The young flower girl lined the path decoratively with white, champagne, and pink rose petals. Next came Carter, the handsome page boy… without his pens!

He was followed by my three nieces, the bridesmaids, dressed in rose-pink, satin, knee-length dresses. Each niece held a hoop-shaped bridal flower wreath made of more white, champagne, and pink roses, with matching floral decoration in their upswept hair.

My arm was linked with my dad, as he escorted his dazzling daughter through the birch arch, with roses and peonies enveloping the open church doors. The delicate fragrance of the freshly-cut flowers filled the air.

The guests looked at me, took pictures of me in my incredible gown and waved at me with smiling faces. A few of them wept, others craning their heads towards me, the bride. My dress created an enchanting movement as I walked purposefully down the aisle, mesmerising and making jaws drop.

Up ahead, my fiancé was waiting patiently for his darling bride. He stood tall with shoulders back and eyes focused on me. As I drew closer, affectionate tears filled his welcoming eyes. I was adorned for my bridegroom.

At the end of the aisle, my dad squeezed my hand, looked into my eyes and smiled jubilantly. He was thankful that he had lived to see this day. He placed my slim cool hand into Jeremy's warm one.

The minister welcomed the guests, 'Please be seated.'

'Dearly beloved, we are gathered here in the presence of God, family and friends to unite Amber and Jeremy in holy matrimony. Marriage is an honourable estate and is, therefore, not to be entered into lightly but reverently, advisedly, soberly and with God's blessing.

Today, they will receive God's greatest gift: another person to share with, grow with, change with, be joyful with and stand with as one, when trials and tribulations enter their lives. It is fitting, therefore, that we should, on this occasion, begin by asking for God's blessing for this marriage. Let us pray.'

He gave a speech, and afterwards, vows were exchanged.

On cue, the best man came forward and presented the rings. Jeremy placed the gold ring on my finger, and then I placed a matching ring on Jeremy's finger.

'By the authority invested in me, I now pronounce you husband and wife. You may now kiss the bride.'

Jeremy was glowing as he placed his arm around my waist, leaned in and kissed me... much more passionately than I was expecting! The guests erupted in cheer, and the minister pried us apart by saying loudly, 'The honeymoon is for later!' A raucous laugh echoed throughout the church. What an unforgettable day!

+ + +

"Take delight in the Lord, and he will give you the desires of your heart."
(Psalm 37:4 NIV).

REFLECTION

- Do you have a dream? Never give up on that dream. Amber had a dream, and it came true. If we seek first the kingdom of God and His righteousness all these things will be given to us. Sometimes God surprises us with good things that are very different to what we had been hoping for.
- The gown was stained, and Jenny had to replace it, as she couldn't wash it out. Are there memories of stains in your life that cling to you? Why not bring them to God in prayer.
- Sometimes we have stains of grief or disappointment in our lives. We long for the day when God will finally put everything right - whether right now, or on the day He has promised when Jesus returns.
- Carter nearly ruined the day for Amber, but Amber's loving sister came to the rescue. At certain times in life, we need someone to stand with us to make our journey in life a little easier. Do you have others who can stand by you? Can you be there to stand with someone else?
- Amber wanted to look glorious for her bridegroom, and with help she succeeded. She looked glamorous and awesome. When she walked down the aisle, people turned their heads with joy and gladness, sharing her dream with her.
- Amber was dressed in a white gown, which symbolises purity. She was coming to her husband as a pure bride. Retaining our purity is very precious, and it's a blessing. It's hard at times but not impossible.

> When we give our lives to Jesus and come to Him, He makes us His bride – indeed, He is preparing His church as a bride, and He is the bridegroom whose return we await. Whatever spots or wrinkles we may have, we have them no more when we are with Him. We stand pure before Him because He has purified us with his self-sacrifice on the cross and by sending His Holy Spirit to dwell in our hearts.

"Let us rejoice and be glad and give Him glory! For the wedding of the Lamb has come, and His bride has made herself ready."
(Revelation 19:7 NIV)

AMBER
The Honeymoon

"...as a bridegroom rejoices over his bride,
so will your God rejoice over you."
(Isaiah 62:5 NIV)

Our long-awaited honeymoon was finally here. I was immensely happy to finally be with the man I loved and adored. Jeremy was all mine.

We landed at the Santorini Airport in Greece, where we waited for hours for our luggage to arrive, only to find that Jeremy's suitcase wasn't in the baggage reclaim area.

We headed over to the baggage kiosk. The airport staff told us that Jeremy's suitcase will be found and sent to our hotel. Jeremy, discouraged, was pushing my four-wheeler suitcase along the smooth floor.

'Oh, Jeremy! Don't worry, it will turn up soon. I'm sure we can buy something suitable for a few days on the island.'

Sighing dramatically, he replied, 'It's terribly disappointing, but hey, we have each other.' His playful smile said it all.

Thankfully, we had brought along a small carry-on suitcase with extra clothing for the both of us, just in case.

Our taxi driver was holding up a card with our names written on as we walked out of customs. He welcomed us to Greece and invited us to begin our journey to our exciting location. We were headed to Hotel Katikies, Santorini in Oia.

'What an amazing view, Jeremy!' I said enthusiastically as we rode in the taxi. 'Look!' I waved and pointed eagerly, grabbing Jeremy's arm as we passed a volcanic site. The refreshing island wind caressed my face through the open window.

We were both mesmerised by the island's beauty and the stunning view of whitewashed houses clinging to the cliffside, with multicoloured cliffs and a perfectly blue sky that matched the glittering sea.

The taxi driver pointed out our hotel from a distance. It was a charming edifice perched on the cliffs overlooking the Aegean Sea.

'Wow, no wonder Oia is famous for its dramatic views,' Jeremy remarked as he peered out the taxi window. 'It doesn't seem real, Amber.'

'I read that Oia is home to enchanting restaurants and diverse shopping centres,' I said cheekily, turning my face towards Jeremy.

'Ladies and their shopping!' He shook his head, grinning.

I laughed heartily, 'It's good therapy... Look, Jeremy! You can see the town. It's etched into the cliffs of the mountains... How divine!'

'It's amazing,' Jeremy agreed.

The taxi driver pulled up at the hotel entrance and helped us with our luggage.

Once we arrived at the reception, we were kindly escorted to our villa.

'Wow!' Jeremy exclaimed in surprise as the porter opened the door and placed our luggage inside on the shiny marble floor.

As the door closed behind us, we scanned the interior admiringly. The room was spacious, bright and clean.

A dinner table was decorated with a beautiful array of tall, fresh and colourful exotic flowers elegantly arranged in a slender, ornate vase. An intricate bowl designed with tiny pearls and brimming with the island's fruits was displayed on the side of the table. A requisite bottle of champagne on ice, accompanied by two flute glasses, was ready for drinking. Small delicacies were scattered around the table. In a corner, near the soft seating area, was a complimentary basket of the location's keepsakes to take home. I loved the paper boats and a patterned scarf.

The amazing room had a white settee and TV, a mini bar and an espresso maker adequately supplied with coffee pods. The bedroom was upstairs, in what the islanders called the loft, facing the sea. We headed up to take a look.

The bright, airy bedroom took our breath away. We gawked in astonishment. It was exquisitely adorned for a honeymoon couple. The bed was made up with gorgeous, luxurious soft lace bedding and a soft pearl-coloured bed throw. A long, plush stool stood at the foot of the bed. Red roses were arranged all around the room; the smell was enchanting.

The delicate artistic work of the ballerina portraits hanging on the walls captured my attention – as a child, I had attended ballet lessons for ten years. The long windows were draped with heavy apricot-coloured curtains tied back, adding more charm to the room.

The king-sized bed itself was sprinkled with dried red and white petals, and immaculate Mr and Mrs towels intricately decorated with white and red ribbon were laid out.

I followed Jeremy back down the stairs saying, 'Darling, I am now Mrs Amber Lees.'

Jeremy's tender gaze was transfixed on me, as if in a dream, realising that this beloved woman before him was truly his wife.

'Let's open the bubbly,' I enthusiastically declared.

Jeremy popped the cork, poured out the cold champagne and handed me a flute.

We exchanged cheeky smiles and clinked our glasses.

'I love you, Amber,' Jeremy said as the cold champagne slid down our throats.

'I love you more!' I replied with a mischievous smile. I let out a sighing breath as I tilted my head back and savoured each swallow of the bubbly.

Placing his flute on the table, Jeremy gently took mine out of my hands and placed it next to his. He stroked my eyebrows with the back of his thumbs, then placed his hands around my chin and pulled me closer towards him.

'God made you for me. He made you so beautiful and pure. He made you to fit perfectly in my arms.'

I wrapped my bare arms around his neck and softly placed a hand on his snow-white hair as he lowered his mouth, taking my lips with his, exploring the passion he had faithfully denied until we were married. I matched him kiss for kiss, pressing closer with deep passionate energy. He kissed me with all the longing he had buried during the months of waiting.

+ + +

The next morning surprised me. Having been single for so long, I was used to having my own space and doing my own thing. So, when Jeremy lounged on the bed, calling my name, I stirred, opened my eyes and jumped out of my skin! Then, the realisation dawned on me... *I'm married!* And this was the first time he had seen me with my hair unbrushed and no makeup.

'I'm so sorry, Jeremy,' pushing myself up and brushing my hair with my fingers. 'I'm so surprised to see another person in the room with me.'

We both laughed wholeheartedly as we embraced each other good morning and shared a quick peck.

I am not a morning person, and I took my time getting out of bed to draw open the curtains.

'Jeremy, you have to see this,' I said enthusiastically, kneeling on the couch that stood against the window, as I glanced back at Jeremy. 'Look at the magnificent sea glistening with the morning sun.' My eyes widened. 'I saw the island on our way here, but I didn't realise we'd have such a view of the sea. How delightful!'

'God has given us the privilege of marvelling at the majestic views of his creation from our terraced villa,' Jeremy said as he joined me at the window, wrapping his arms around my waist. 'They say the islands were built by the volcanic eruptions. Isn't it grand, Amber?'

I leaned back into his embrace, mesmerised by what I saw before me. I couldn't help but gaze in wonder. 'We have our own private hot tub too, I almost forgot. We can enjoy it later this evening.'

'While we sip champagne,' Jeremy whispered softly. He gently brushed his bearded face against mine as his arms tightened around me.

Placing a delicate kiss on my neck, and spanking me on the butt, 'Go get dressed, Amber, so we can go for breakfast.'

'OK Mr Lees,' I smiled, and got down from the couch.

'I saw that they have international foods as well as local cuisine on the menu. I'm famished,' Jeremy said.

I quickly showered and dressed in a cotton floral-print midi dress. Jeremy wore loose grey trousers and a white T-shirt.

The morning was already hot, hotter than I had expected. We needed to go shopping after breakfast as Jeremy had only one more outfit to wear from the carry-on suitcase.

We were escorted to our breakfast table by a kind-faced waiter. We sat near the buffet table, which pleased Jeremy. As we settled down, a middle-aged woman stared in our direction. I was sure she was staring at Jeremy. We were about to scrutinise the buffet, when she paraded down the aisle elegantly, heading towards us.

Her pearl-white skin and dusty-brown hair complimented her soft blush-pink chiffon dress. The bodice clung to her – she was well endowed. Her hair was curiously arranged with two dagger-like combs flashing with jewels. A single jewel shone at her throat on an invisible chain, and jewels flashed from her wrists right down to her crimson heels. The whole effect was startling. Who was this evidently rich woman?

'Jeremy... darling,' she slurred, 'I thought it was you.' She extended her arms for an embrace.

Flustered, Jeremy tried to collect himself. 'Lydia, how... how... wonderful to... to see you.' He stood up to accept and reciprocate her embrace. 'What... what are you doing here?'

'That's a nice way to greet a long-lost friend.'

'Excuse me. This is my wife, Amber.'

'Your wife!' She looked me up and down, as if to size me up.

I rose from my seat, 'Pleased to meet you,' I said, extending my hand and inhaling her overbearing perfume.

'The pleasure is all mine,' she replied with a plastic smile.

'Amber, this is Lydia, an old friend of the family. Lydia, of all the places to meet, I can't believe you're here.'

'Neither can I, darling,' she echoed in an alluringly sultry voice.

'We're on our honeymoon.'

'Honeymoon? How wonderful,' she said in a forced tone. 'Jeremy, it must be... eight years since I last saw you.'

'Umm, more than that I think, Lydia. Where's Derek?'

She tilted her head down. 'Unfortunately, he died two years ago.'

'I'm so sorry... He was a good man. So... you're... here alone?'

'Yes... Do you mind if I join you?'

Raising an eyebrow, Jeremy answered, 'Not at all, how rude of me. We were just going to get breakfast, we'll be back shortly. Do take a seat.' Jeremy pulled out a chair for her. 'Can I get you something?'

'Just coffee, please,' she replied, placing her bag on the marble floor.

We strolled hand in hand towards the buffet table. 'What a surprise to see Lydia here,' Jeremy remarked.

'Yes, indeed,' I said uncertainly.

'Lydia was my deceased wife's friend. When I lost Jill, Lydia and her husband, Derek, were there to support me. Derek was a rock when I needed one.'

'I remember you saying you moved closer to your family and friends after Jill died.'

'That's right,' he replied, glancing at the buffet and wondering what to have first. 'But then I lost contact with them. I didn't even know Derek is no longer with us.' Lowering his voice he added, 'I hope you didn't mind me asking her to join us?'

'It's OK. She was Jill's friend and your close friend's wife. She was there in your time of need.'

We returned to the table with our plates overflowing and Jeremy's stomach rumbling. The breakfast was delightful. The only downside was the conversation, which flowed only two ways; Jeremy and Lydia certainly had much catching up to do.

After breakfast, Jeremy and I went shopping. During the conversation over breakfast, Lydia had skilfully managed to weasel her way into joining us on our shopping trip. I thought nothing of it. She was by herself and lonely, and we had an enjoyable day checking out the shops and tasting the local cuisine. Lydia was good company too, and Jeremy bought more than he needed. *And I thought women liked to shop!*

The next day, we had a boat tour booked, and the coach was scheduled to leave for Athinios Port at noon. I was excited about the day's trip, and so was Jeremy. We got dressed and went for a late breakfast. Lydia had been looking for us. Jeremy and Lydia got chatting at the breakfast table, and as we ate and conversed, we completely lost track of the time. Finally, we realised that our tour coach would be waiting for us.

We rushed to our villa, made a quick bathroom stop, grabbed our belongings and hurried to the coach pickup point.

The tour guide spoke to us when we arrived, 'What time do you call this? The coach should have left at 12noon,' Lifting his arm to view his watch, 'It's 12.15pm!'

'We're so so sorry,' said Jeremy.

'You've taken time from the other tourists,' he added as we found our seats.

I was too embarrassed and kept my head low.

'Don't worry, we won't miss the boat!' said a passenger, as the coach started to move.

When we arrived at Athinios Port, we had to choose between climbing down steep steps, riding on a donkey to the bottom, or taking a cable car to reach the shore. As we were already late, all of us decided we had better walk down the steps.

I didn't realise how unfit I was until I got to the bottom, over one hundred and seventy steps later, panting. My legs were shaking. All I wanted to do was to sit. Jeremy and I, as well as most of the coach party, relaxed by sitting on the wall that stood on the sandy beach while we waited for our boat.

Suddenly, someone approached us, wading through the sand. I couldn't believe my eyes. It was Lydia! *How did she get here so quickly?*

As if reading my mind, she said, 'I already had a taxi waiting for me and forgot to tell you during our conversation that I, too, was booked onto this trip.'

Somehow, I didn't believe her.

As usual, the day had started off extremely warm and then became almost scorching. There wasn't a cloud in the sky and no breeze. I reached intently into my bag to pull out my sunscreen lotion, as Jeremy had forgotten to apply it on himself. Lydia and I were sitting on either side of Jeremy on the wall. The boat was now running late. The next thing I knew, Lydia was rubbing sunscreen lotion onto Jeremy's arm.

What is she doing? He's my husband! I swallowed and blinked a few times, I didn't want to lose control. My face tightened as if all my facial muscles were holding in my emotions.

'I used to do this for Derek. I hope you don't mind, Jeremy, but you really do need to make sure you are well protected from the sun.'

'I mind, Lydia! He's my husband!' I blurted out.

'Oh, I'm so sorry,' she said, her hands dropping. 'I was forgetting my place.'

Jeremy frowned. A moment of uneasy awkward silence followed.

Jeremy turned his head towards me, glaring at me. I was wrong to say what I was thinking.

Twenty minutes later, the boat finally arrived. It wasn't as full as we had expected.

Our first stop was Palea Kameni, where Jeremy took the plunge and soaked in the naturally heated pools with most of the tourists. I can't swim so stayed on board. I settled at a table on the deck, taking in the natural scenery and keeping an eye focussed on Jeremy. I was happy to see him relaxing. But as I watched him from the boat, I noticed those dagger-combs flashing as Lydia swam towards him. I wanted to relax and enjoy myself and my husband – three was definitely too crowded!

About half an hour later, Jeremy came back on board. I was seething. *God, you have to help me.*

'Jeremy, did you have a good time?' I tried so hard to keep my anger at bay.

'Yes, it was invigorating and pretty hot too. Glad I had the sunscreen lotion on,' he replied matter-of-factly, drying himself with a bath towel, as if nothing was wrong.

'I noticed you were with "dagger comb".'

'Dagger who?' he asked.

I folded my arms crossly. 'Lydia!'

'Have I done something wrong?' he asked, turning and frowning at me.

'You seemed to be having a very nice conversation with her, while I was here alone on the boat.'

'Darling, it was just a friendly chat… Don't tell me you're jealous?'

'Jealous?!' My voice rose an octave. I realised where I was and lowered my head. 'Darling, I just can't see why she has to be everywhere we seem to go. I want to enjoy your company and be able to relax without having to look over my shoulder to see what you're up to with her.'

Hitting the towel on the table, 'Amber! That's enough.' We locked eyes. 'There's no need for you to be jealous or worried about anything. I'm your husband. It's you I married, and it's you I'm in love with, not Lydia. I have no interest in Lydia whatsoever.' He seated himself next to me overlooking the sea and, picking up the towel, continued to dry his legs.

I rested my hands on the tabletop to avoid fidgeting. 'Are you sure she has no interest in you?' I asked, adjusting my hat against the beating sun.

'Don't be ridiculous! Of course, she hasn't. She knows we're married.'

'If she's a good person, then why is she always hanging around us?' I asked.

Jeremy flung his towel to one side. 'She is on her own and looking for company. As I said, Derek, her husband, was good to me. Surely we can return that favour.'

That made me feel guilty. 'I guess so...' I murmured. I lowered my head and looked out to sea. 'I'm sorry, darling.'

Smiling, he tilted my head and pulled me towards him. 'It's you I love...'

Just as he was about to kiss me, a loud voice called out, 'Yoohoo! It's me...'

She even had to spoil that intimate moment.

'Jeremy, would you be a darling and help me walk towards a seat?' Lydia called. 'I think I've sprained my ankle slightly.'

'Sure.'

I shuffled uncomfortably in my seat as Jeremy dashed to her rescue.

Lydia wrapped a sky-blue towel around her waist and fetched her belongings. She reached decisively for her sunscreen lotion, located in her beach bag, and massaged it into her shoulders… I knew what was coming…

'Jeremy, would you be a darling and help me rub the cream on the back of my shoulders and back? I think I have a bit of arthritis in one shoulder, and I'm struggling.' Her captivating, sophisticated voice was hard to resist.

'No problem.'

I have a problem.

I so wanted to leave my seat and rub the lotion somewhere else on Lydia. How dare she! *God forgive me for that evil thought.*

Lydia glanced at me with a sly smile. 'Amber, you should've come and joined us in the water… It was so relaxing and good for my arthritis. They say the water has sulphur, iron and other minerals… Are you all right, Amber? You look a bit… faint.'

'I'm fine, Lydia,' I rasped, forcing a smile for Jeremy's sake. 'Maybe it's just the sun, it's extremely hot.' I reached for my fan, which was lying on the table, and rapidly fanned my face as I stared in disbelief at them.

'Yes, it is awfully hot,' she said, rolling her shoulders as Jeremy continued to massage them. 'Thank you, Jeremy.' She tilted her head back to behold his face. 'That feels good already.'

I looked away before I said something I would regret, fanning myself with one hand and pretending to inspect my newly done acrylic nails on the other.

Our next stop was the volcano. I couldn't wait to arrive there. Listening to the tour operator took my mind off the earlier event.

Before we descended from the boat, we made sure to take plenty of drinking water for the climb up the soil path to the crater of the still active volcano. I knew that somehow Lydia would be a part of our company, so I prepared myself. And much to my disappointment, she was.

There was absolutely no shade on the volcano, so I was glad for my hat and my cotton shawl to cover my shoulders. The volcano didn't look like it was active, but rather like a planet – except for the fumaroles. It was a fifteen-minute walk to the top of the volcano. Lydia couldn't manage it and asked Jeremy to escort her. My entire day seemed ruined. I was on the verge of tears.

Our next stop was to eat at Thirasia and explore the area for an hour and a half and then watch the spectacular sunset in Oia.

Oia is famous for its beautiful sunsets, and I couldn't wait for Jeremy and I to sit and watch the sun disappear into the sea together. However, I knew in my heart that we would have company, so again, I prepared myself. And lo and behold, Lydia was there, taking Jeremy's attention and ignoring me.

When we arrived back at the villa after what seemed to have been a strenuous day, Jeremy and I had words.

My head was wet with perspiration as I flung my hat onto the settee. Thank goodness the air conditioning was cool and welcoming.

'Jeremy, let's talk,' I said, trying to keep the hurt out of my voice.

'Talk about what, darling?' he asked, as his eyes looked deep into mine.

We were interrupted by a knock on the door. *Not again*, I thought, placing a hand on my hip. Thankfully, it was the porter, Jeremy's suitcase had arrived.

'I'm so glad my case is here.' He pulled it into the room. 'Darling, you said you wanted to talk… Now I can dress up for dinner with my superwoman tomorrow,' he said elatedly as he knelt and opened the case.

'I want to talk about Lydia.' At this point, both my hands were on my hips.

'Lydia?' Jeremy was surprised that I mentioned her name and heard my slow intake of breath.

'Jeremy, this is the second day of our honeymoon, and Lydia has been everywhere with us. I wanted you to myself, not to have someone else tagging along…' I choked.

'Oh, darling,' he sighed as he rose and pulled me into a cuddle.

'I don't want you to be upset…' rubbing my back. 'Remember Derek and Lydia have done a lot for me. I don't expect you to understand.' He reached for my hands.

'I know you feel a sense of obligation to her due to Derek… and…'

Tears slid down my face. Jeremy tried to wipe my cheeks with his fingers, but new tears tumbled down before he could brush the old ones away. His dreamy eyes captivated me, and I broke out in a smile.

'Come here,' he said.

I placed my arms around his tanned neck, hoping he would pay attention and listen. 'Jeremy...'

His tender arms made their way to my waist. Gently, he pulled me towards him, nibbling my lips.

'No! Listen first...'

He rained light kisses all over my face and kissed my neck softly before making his way back towards my lips.

'Jeremy... listen... Je...re...my...' I trailed off as I melted into his warm embrace. I could not resist his heavenly lips. He was mine.

+ + +

'I'm off for my massage this morning, remember?' I said to Jeremy.

'Yeah, that's fine. I'll just relax outside on the patio, catching up on our local newspaper until you come back. Then we can stroll down the road to the local shops.'

'That sounds great. Love you,' I said, planting a quick kiss on his lips.

'Love you more,' was his quirky response. 'Missing you already...' His bubbly tone overflowed with affection.

Once I arrived at the massage parlour, I realised I had left my token in the villa. The masseuse said I could bring it later, to pay for the massage, but I said I'd just go back and get it as it would only take me five minutes and she did not have a customer booked in after me.

At the villa, I fumbled with my key at the door. When I finally opened it, there were Lydia and Jeremy in an embrace.

'What's going on?' I demanded angrily.

'Amber! Lydia was upset and...'

'I was the one who went into Jeremy's arms for comfort,' she moved towards me.

'This is too much. Lydia, please leave now,' I said, irritated.

'Amber!' exclaimed Jeremy. 'It was an innocent embrace.'

'Had I not come in when I did, what else would it have been?'

'Nothing,' said Jeremy, waving his arms.

Lydia strolled back towards Jeremy and touched his arm, 'Amber, you are overexaggerating. Jeremy is right, it was a harmless embrace. I was upset.'

'You were upset... *You* were upset?!' I stood with my back against the door. 'What do you think *I* am, Lydia, stupid? This is our honeymoon, not yours. Now, please leave,' I said firmly.

'I can see you're upset, Amber, but you've got this whole situation wrong.'

'Have I, Lydia? I told you to leave... Now...'

She took her shawl, gaped at Jeremy, gave me a dirty look as I moved out of the way and left, slamming the door behind her.

Tears welled up without warning, and I broke down. 'Jeremy, this is supposed to be our honeymoon, it should be one of the best times of our lives. I know that Lydia is your friend and that you feel obligated to her, but surely you know this has gone too far.'

'Amber, you are taking this whole thing out of context. She's harmless.' He walked towards me, his arms stretched out to embrace me.

I raised my hands to stop him. 'Please don't touch me... Not right now...'

'Oh, Amber. I'm so sorry...' I heard the hurt in his voice.

'Lydia is a woman.' I rushed to the table, tears coursing down my cheeks, and my hand trembled as I grabbed a tissue.

'What do you mean?' Jeremy asked.

Mopping my tears, I stood glaring into Jeremy's face but new tears tumbled down before I could dry the old ones away. 'Jeremy,' I sobbed, 'she has designs on you. She wants you!'

'Don't be absurd!' he bellowed. 'I have told you before, I am married to you, not her!'

'She's flirting with you, Jeremy! I can't take it anymore.' I stomped around the room.

'Darling...' Jeremy entreated, grabbing my arms to stop me. 'You've got this all wrong. She's a good friend...'

'And I am your wife! I am more than a good friend,' I retorted, looking him right in the eye. 'I'm off to the parlour.' I had completely forgotten that the reason I came back to the villa was to get the token. I turned on my heels and quickly made my way out the door.

'Amber...' I heard Jeremy's voice behind me as he followed me out the door.

I sprinted away to the parlour, tears pouring down my cheeks. *This is our honeymoon...! Father God, please help me.*

Fighting back my tears, I suddenly turned around and returned to the villa, opened the door, found Jeremy and said, 'And… and don't let me find dagger-comb here when I return!'

'Amber! Her name is Lydia.'

'Arrh… Don't get me started, Jeremy!' Slamming the door, I left and walked dazed back to the parlour, leaving Jeremy alone.

The massage was relaxing, but I couldn't help but think about Lydia and why Jeremy couldn't see what kind of woman she was. It was unbearable. After I left the parlour, I went to sit in a quiet corner, alone… In the silence, the words "Love your neighbour as yourself" came to me. I sat there pondering, looking out at the turquoise sea that seemed limitless – how mighty and peaceful it was – and prayed. I had to trust God to sort this out for me… Jeremy was a man of prayer and I knew in my heart he would have been praying to our heavenly Father.

Finally, I returned to the villa. When Jeremy saw my face was red and swollen from crying, a pained look swept over him. He pulled me to him and stroked my silky hair. I hiccupped against his T-shirt, trying to catch my breath. His arms tightened around me as I clung to him.

'I'm so sorry darling. Please forgive me?'

I nodded and clung closer to him.

'Everything will be OK... I promise.'

+ + +

For the next two days, Lydia was nowhere to be seen. But I still couldn't relax, always wanting to look over my shoulder to see if she was nearby. I decided to visit her at her villa. I told Jeremy I was going to make another appointment with the massage parlour, which I was, but I went to find Lydia first.

I had no idea which villa was hers and had to go to the reception desk to find out. The staff at the desk promptly told me - they had seen us together and probably thought we were friends.

My knock on her door went unanswered. *I wonder where she could be?*

I had started to write a note when I heard humming. Lydia was in. I knocked on the door again. This time, she opened it. She was surprised to see me. She was dressed in a light orange oversized shirt with open toe slippers.

'Oh, it's you,' she said sarcastically.

'Can I have a word with you, Lydia?'

She hesitated for a moment before saying, 'Do come in.' Her tone had changed, she sounded genuine and warm.

Her villa was similar to ours but more spacious.

Before I had time to speak, she asked in her refined voice, 'Does Jeremy know you're here?'

'No, he doesn't.'

'Why are you here, Amber?'

We stood facing each other.

'I thought that was obvious. I love Jeremy. I have waited a long time to be married, and finally, I have found the one who loves me and whom I love. Everything was going well until you came on the scene. I don't want to fight, Lydia. This is our honeymoon.'

Lydia tilted her head and looked at me silently before turning and strolling over to a nearby table. She picked up a cigarette, slipped it between her lipstick-coated lips and lit it. Closing her eyes, she took a long inhale before blowing the smoke out of her mouth.

Complete silence filled the room as she continued to drag in the fumes.

Then, she turned to face me. 'Amber, I did everything possible to win your husband away from you. I wanted a man in my life, and I remembered how Jeremy was a gentleman – he certainly still is. You're a lucky woman to have him. He is very much in love with you.'

I stood still, shocked by her honesty.

'I understand that it must be hard being single again after you had a good marriage.'

'You have no idea, Amber, how lonely it is and how much you want to recreate what you had,' Lydia said, stamping the cigarette out.

'This is my first marriage. My only marriage.'

'I know, and I shouldn't have done what I did.' She moved towards a chair and sat down heavily. 'I was so desperate for someone to love me and to be loved again...'

I walked over to the chair next to her and sat, reaching out a hand to touch her arm. 'I understand, Lydia... and I'm sorry for any unkind words I said to you.'

'Forget it. I deserved it. You were angry, fighting for your man! I like that in you... Besides, I'm going home soon.'

'Home?' I asked, leaning forward.

'Yes, late tomorrow afternoon.'

'Oh.'

'Can I pop by and say goodbye to Jeremy?'

I hesitated before smiling. 'Yes, you can. Why don't you walk back with me?'

Lydia thought about it for a moment. 'Sounds like a good idea. Let me change quickly.'

As we ambled back to the villa together, Lydia was very pleasant. I saw a side of her I hadn't seen before. Jeremy had gone out, perhaps for a newspaper, as he liked to know what was going on back home.

Lydia and I talked and laughed together. I was surprised to find that deep down, Lydia was a kind person. It was good to hear about her childhood, her challenges in life and how she had met Derek.

When our conversation slowed, Lydia came over to me and gave me a hug, saying she was sorry for being a fool. I reciprocated her warm embrace.

Just then, Jeremy walked in. 'Oh, have I got something to worry about?'

We all chuckled.

'We were just sorting something out that should have been sorted out a while ago,' I said, smiling with Lydia, her eyes warm and kind.

'I'm glad you ladies are getting on. I have a wonderful surprise.'

'Oh, what is it, Jeremy?' I asked excitedly.

'I won a prize from the games evening.'

'How wonderful!' Lydia exclaimed. 'OK, tell us what prize you won.'

'Dinner for four at the most expensive restaurant on the island with local entertainment.'

'Wow!' I gasped, clasping my hands together.

'By the way,' said Lydia, 'I came by to let you know that I'm leaving tomorrow.'

'You are?' Jeremy replied with a sad smile.

'Yes, it's time for me to go. I wish you both all the happiness in the world.'

Tears welled up in my eyes and Lydia's – the first outward sign of emotion I had seen from her.

'What time are you leaving?' Jeremy asked.

'Not until late tomorrow afternoon.'

'What are you doing this evening?'

'Nothing, as I've already packed.'

'I have four tickets...'

'Oh yes, do come, Lydia!' I entreated joyously.

'Well... It's a date!'

We had a wonderful evening, with Jeremy dressed up in his exquisitely cut tuxedo, a perfect match for his suave manners, and Lydia and I dressed elegantly – we did not outdo each other.

'Lydia, let's keep in touch,' I said sincerely as we embraced again.

'I'd like that.'

That night, it was sad to see Lydia go.

+ + +

The next day, we received a telephone call from the reception desk to say an important message was waiting for us. We had hoped to see Lydia at breakfast, but we found out that she had left early.

"My dear friends,

I know I have taken up so much of your precious time, and I am grateful to both of you for allowing me to accompany you. I stole precious moments away from you, I hope this little contribution will make up for it.

Thank you for trusting me, Jeremy. When you signed paperwork for me, you were signing to say that you were willing to change your flights! I took the liberty of changing your flights and adding an extra three days to your honeymoon, all paid for. I know you didn't see all the island, so I have also arranged extra excursions for you with some of the best restaurants on the island. I have also paid for you both to have a joint spa session. You deserve the best. Hope you have enough clothes!

Lydia."

'Wow... I never saw this coming!' Jeremy exclaimed.

'Neither did I.'

'She is some lady...'

'She certainly is,' shaking my head. 'Let's pray for Lydia, Jeremy.'

We walked back to our villa and, once inside, knelt to pray.

'God, this honeymoon wasn't what I expected, but thank you for the lessons I have learnt through it. Thank you for Lydia.

Give her a friend that she can do things with. Bless her for her kindness to us,' I prayed.

Jeremy continued, 'Father God, she's such a great lady who needs you. Show her your love and compassion. And thank you for giving me the best wife ever. Amen.'

'Amen,' I echoed with a warm smile.

'It would be nice to go for a walk on the beach today, just the two of us, since we have no tours,' I suggested.

Jeremy's dreamy eyes met mine, as they shone like dark gems; I knew what that meant...

'Here we go again... All these kisses, Jeremy,' I protested playfully as he pressed kisses into my hair and trailed butterfly kisses down my neck.

Before his tender lips met mine, he whispered softly, 'We are... on our honeymoon!'

REFLECTION

Being married doesn't mean that trials and tribulations do not come. This was only the beginning of Amber and Jeremy's future, and Amber did not foresee this happening on her honeymoon. When things went wrong, she turned to God.

WORDS OF WISDOM

In life, plans don't always go the way we expect them to, but through prayer and leaving our problems with God, things can turn out better than we intended.

EPILOGUE
The Nail

... I once was lost but now I'm found;
was blind but now I see.
(Taken from Amazing Grace by John Newton,
and John 9:25 NIV)

What being a slave means:

You have no authority, no rights nor power to control your destiny. In the eyes of the world, you are worthless. You are someone else's property and own nothing.

"The Spirit of the Lord is on me,
because he has anointed me
to proclaim good news to the poor.
He has sent me to proclaim freedom for the prisoners
and recovery of sight for the blind,
to set the oppressed free,
to proclaim the year of the Lord's favour."
(Luke 4:18-19 NIV)

+ + +

Born innocent, yet I stood like a criminal, motionless, on a rickety wooden platform. My ankles hurt, shackled down by a rusty old chain. My hands and neck were restrained with heavy metal cuffs.

Wrenched from my family, I had been stolen into slavery. A weary disbelief engulfed me; after toiling under half a dozen masters already, I was to be sold all over again. When would this end?

As my turn in the auction grew near, I frantically looked around. Imposing buildings encircled the sweltering market square. There was nowhere to run, nowhere to hide, no one to turn to in desperation.

My heart raced like a runaway train, thumping so hard against my rib cage that it could easily erupt. My mouth was parched from the dusty road. I thirsted for a cool drink of water. I was burning beneath the blazing sun. I dared not wipe my brow. Sweat poured down like water streaming down leaves in a thunderstorm.

Fifteen other slaves stood in a row alongside me - male and female, young and middle-aged. We were all completely stripped of clothing. We were exposed to the sneering stares of the market, we couldn't hide our shame.

I hung my head in humiliation while people appraised my naked frame standing on the hard auction platform. Splinters dug into my right foot.

'Hold your head up, you wretch!' With a jolt of adrenaline like lightning down my spine, I obeyed the hoarsely shouted command.

Children passed by, laughing at me, pointing their skinny fingers in my direction as if I were an animal hung for sport. Men looked at me with leering, sickening eyes. Anxiously, I waited for someone to purchase me. *Purchase me!* I shivered from head to toe, teeth chattering from the fear of not knowing who my next master would be. Surely they couldn't treat me worse than this? How long should I suffer this trepidation?

A gentleman strode across to the slave market carrying a nail. He appeared to be from out of town. The busy crowd was also scrutinising him – though they afforded him more respect and dignity than they did us. He was impeccably dressed in a white linen suit, so white I was sure it shone. An air of grace and authority emanated from him.

Without flinching, he nodded to the salesman and said, 'I want to buy all the slaves.' He named his price.

The wrinkled salesman's bulging stomach bounced up and down as he stood laughing hysterically, holding his cigar between his fingers. With a piercing look at the stranger he grinned, 'You must be joking! These slaves aren't worth it! Are you crazy?!'

The man with the nail responded, 'They're worth it to me.' His voice was surprisingly gentle yet firm. I was amazed. It seemed he really meant it. His gracious words were a breath of fresh air in the stench of the sweaty market.

The salesman wobbled and limped slowly to the seat, near to the wooden platform, tilted his head towards the man with the nail, and leant forward. 'What's your business?'

'To do the will of my Father who sent me. His business requires as many slaves as possible.'

'You don't say,' the salesman said, slurring his words as he reached for his cigar from between his thin lips. He glanced quizzically at the nail the man held and placed the thick cigar back into his open mouth.

'Sir,' the salesman retorted, 'It's an extremely high price. Don't get me wrong, I'll gladly take your charity, but no one has paid... *no one*... this amount for these slaves before. You serious?'

'Yes I am.'

'Alright. You got yourself a deal, Mister.'

The man with the nail redeemed us and took us with him, without inspecting his merchandise like the others had done with their cruel, callous glares. We were loaded into a cart pulled by four well-groomed white stallion horses.

Now that we sat opposite each other in rows, I noticed one of the female slaves, Megan, was badly disfigured, probably from being beaten by her former slave owner. Thank God the new Master had bought her. Without a buyer, she would have been dragged away and left to die deep in some dark wood.

Once out of sight of the slave market we came to a gentle stop – the stallions were well trained. The man with the nail gave us clean wraps to cover our naked bodies. How strange! We were filthy and reeking, Megan shuffled uncomfortably and became sick all over herself.

'Don't worry Megan,' said Viola next to her, 'he can't be as bad as the last one – and I've got your back.' She clasped a reassuring hand on her knee.

'Thanks,' she whispered back, 'I hope you're right.'

The man with the nail came over and unshackled us all one by one. Why had he personally taken it upon himself to do this? Any other owner would leave us shackled until we arrived, and even then would leave one slave to unshackle the rest.

He knelt beside me. In his soft smile, I sensed tenderness and care.

'We won't be needing that,' he said warmly, as he creaked open the binds on my neck, hands and ankles. The touch of his hand against my skin sent ripples of adoration through me. It didn't matter to him how we looked. Even I could still smell our stench, yet it didn't bother him in the least. He treated us differently. Surely, he didn't care for us slaves? I had heard others whisper there could be a good master out there somewhere and now I was starting to believe this.

Standing again, the man with the nail looked around at us, eye to eye. 'I have bought your freedom,' he said, 'You are no longer slaves.'

None of us was convinced. Most of us had been slaves more years than we could count and now we were being told we were free?!

'What trick was this?' Samuel muttered beside me, then finding the confidence to call out, 'Why are you toying with us, Master?'

Strangely enough, he spoke in a way I had never been spoken to before. Love echoed from his lips with every word he uttered, 'If you believe in my words, you will know the truth and the truth will set you free.'

He had unlocked my chains. Even chains I didn't know I was carrying suddenly fell off, because my heart was free. A burden was removed from me. I was free! I knew in my heart this was true but I couldn't explain how this had happened. *Believe in his words?* Surely, the man with the nail didn't have anything to do with this.

As the others dared to ask their questions, the man gently answered each one, I stared in wonder into his delightful eyes, which were beaming in the sunlight. His face was glowing with mercy and grace. I knew, in my heart, this Master was different to those I had known previously.

'But will we have to work your fields?' I asked.

'Only if you want to, for a pay. There is plenty of work to be done, and my Father is very generous.'

Peace overwhelmed my very being. My heart leapt with adoration. How wonderful to have a good Master! The other slaves also saw he was a good man.

Free of our shackles, he gave us some clean water to drink. I drank deeply and satisfied my thirst. We then continued our ride.

We journeyed for hours. The pounding heat faded into pleasant warmth. The shadows stretched and yawned. I wasn't scared.

Some time later, when the mid-afternoon sky was clear blue and streaked with paint-brush strokes of fine cloud, we climbed a hill and a stunning view was unveiled below us. It had the hallmarks of an undisturbed paradise. Never had I seen a place so majestically stunning and refreshing.

A cheerful song grew loud to our right, and we gasped in astonishment at a fearsome waterfall, glittering in the last light of the day. The waterfall led to a winding river, flowing through the wide valley beneath us. This lush, enchanting countryside sparkled with shimmering light from up above.

'Pull up here,' the Master instructed, as we approached the river.

'You can dip your toes if you like, or even jump right in! Yes, really, go on! The water is lovely.'

I ran barefoot to the riverbank like a free child, forgetting my pain, and waded quickly towards the waterfall. It was heavenly. I stood under the flow of inviting water, embracing its coolness washing over my head and down my whole body. The thrilling sound was like chiming bells ringing harmoniously around me. It gave me goose bumps.

Beside the riverbank, fragrant flowers gently nodded their resplendent colours towards me in the breeze. As we bathed, we heard frogs croaking and birds melodically singing their evening chorus as if directly to us. Were we dreaming?

Samuel was swimming doing a butterfly stroke, I had no idea he could do that because I had never seen him swim before. Tom was climbing a branch overhanging the water, about to jump in. Never had any of us experienced freedom like this... I could not explain this sweet emotion.

I marvelled at the beautiful pure crystal river, its surface like glass. I felt different: brand new, born again, a new creature. Everything I had suffered from before was completely washed away in the twinkling of an eye - shame, nakedness, hurts, disappointments, bitterness, unforgiveness, hatred, wounds, sorrow, grief, pain, trauma, sicknesses, sores, mental anguish, sexual abuse, abandonment, disgrace, loneliness, fearfulness, the lack of love... The weight of every wrong against me, and even every wrong I had done, vanished. At that moment, I knew I was pure. I couldn't explain this new joy.

As we waded back and rose up the riverbank, a strikingly beautiful woman, whom none of us recognised, came out of the river with us.

Viola whispered, 'Who is she? I don't recognise her from the marketplace.'

'Why are you all staring at me? Do I have something on my face?'

As she spoke, as bewildered as the rest of us, I was absolutely astonished. It was Megan, the disfigured woman I noticed on the cart. Except she wasn't disfigured any more... now she was whole!

She wiped her face to get whatever it was off and found nothing – just skin as new and smooth as a baby's. The scarring was healed. Her jaw dropped open, speechless.

What was it about this place? What was in the water? What was it about that peculiar man? I stared in awe and amazement, pondering who the man with the nail truly was.

After our time in the river, the Master gave everyone fresh laundered towels and brilliantly white garments to wear.

'These robes are yours to wear and keep,' the Master explained, 'a gift from my Father.'

I had never had anything new. His Father must be as kind as him. As I held my long and modest apparel against my chest, my heart danced with joy. I would cherish this gift. No one had ever cared for me like this. The robe was to me a symbol of all the care and gentleness this strange man with a nail had shown today. Tears stung my eyes to know I had something that was mine, and I knew the Master would not take it away from me. I believed his words.

My heart longed to know more about this mysterious Master. When I put my new garment on it was like a shield of protection around me. I was safe and sheltered. I touched it reverently and folded my arms around my body, feeling its softness against my cleansed skin. I closed my eyelids, drinking in the serenity and protection – only momentarily, yet it seemed like a lifetime.

'I bought you for a price. Now that your price has been paid,' the Master said peacefully as he looked into our eyes in turn, 'you are set free. You are warmly invited to stay with me and my Father, or you can return to town, or go wherever you wish. You are free now. You are free, indeed.'

Yes, I was free, indescribably free. The world was mine to explore – and what I wanted to learn most was more about this man, and that nail, and who his Father was.

The Master walked with us up the bank. He led us to a spot beside the road, where an oblong table had been set before us in this open paradise... I hadn't noticed it when we arrived. Someone must have come and decorated it. A colourful centrepiece filled with a colossal flower bouquet had been placed on the white linen tablecloth. I used to serve tables at banquets for my previous master, and the finery here was more exquisite and refined: gold cutlery, stately wine goblets, gold ringed plates and bowls.

A tall, clear glass of red juice awaited each of us. We sat ourselves down and a sudden silence fell as we eagerly sipped the inviting drinks. Lost in a moment of fine flavour, all chatter had been put on pause. I wanted to gulp it down but had learnt to rein myself in to share with other slaves in comradery, to help us survive together. The drink tasted unearthly... the best I have ever had. The fragrance of freshly baked bread added to the peaceful ambience. Yet more delicious foods, with aromas I had never smelt before, were graciously laid before us. I tore my eyes away from the wonderous dishes to thank the server, but words got caught in my throat. The Master was serving us, himself! He smiled sweetly, while I hurried to regain composure.

+ + +

The cooked salmon, rainbow trout and flatfish were covered in delicious herbs, and the serving platters were dressed with huge vegetables and colourful salads. The seasoned chicken legs, breasts, roasted lamb and fragrant rice were bountiful, and all had been brought to us by the generous Master.

What a great feast! I didn't know how long this would last, so I delved in without dithering to enjoy this breath-taking moment of vibrant colours and mouth-watering ripe fruit. It all tasted divine. Savouring a tender mouthful of the roasted lamb, I surveyed the others around me. They were also eating as if it were their last supper.

We were treated like royalty.

I ate until I was full with succulent food and overflowing with pure happiness. I licked my fingers one by one in sheer delight. As the meal drew to an end, we all suddenly burst out into laughter for no reason, without a care in the world, including the Master! He smiled at us and with us. He was pleased we were all happy.

'I want you to follow me,' the Master joyfully said with a twinkle in his eye. We willingly followed. Rising from the banquet, we strolled on along the road, winding through the beautiful valley. We dipped down into lush grove of trees, then back up again as the valley turned eastward. As we walked, a most incredible mansion came into view, sat beautifully on gentle rising hills. Never had I witnessed a great house like this one.

The Master paused at the open gate and turned back to us. From his satchel, he drew out a golden key for each of us, placing them gently into our palms. It was then I saw the scar marks on his hands. I wasn't sure what all this was about.

'These are keys to my mansion. My Father would like to adopt each one of you into our family. You can become my brothers and sisters and share all we have.'

I glanced at the others, who were also bewildered. Who was this Father? What did this all mean?

'Are we your slaves?' Samuel asked in disbelief.

'Sir, what have we done to deserve this? We have nothing to pay you back with,' said Viola.

Understanding shone in his eyes and, smiling, he answered us, 'There is nothing left for you to pay. There is nothing you can do to pay me back... the price has been paid in full.'

We were all silent, hungering for more of his words.

'No longer are you slaves. I have bought you for a price and your freedom is a gift. I know it feels alien right now, but renew your thinking. Let this new reality sink in. You have carried many burdens for many years. Now you can lay them down because I offer you rest. Truly I tell you, you are no longer slaves.'

Then and there I knew I trusted him. We continued up the front path, and I opened the door with my key. Stepping in, I dared not believe my eyes.

'Ever since you bought us,' I said, with a new confidence, 'we have felt different. We have never experienced this joy on earth. You have treated us like kings and queens and now you have given us each a key to your own home! But I don't understand – why?'

The Master turned his face towards mine and gazed at me with deep affection. 'Everything I have done for you is because I love you.'

+ + +

Gazing around the magnificent entrance hall I eagerly peeked inside from the doorway at the beauty displayed, which was only one of many rooms. I ventured in, seeing the glory and majesty of what was truly ours!

Everything I would ever need or desire in life was in the room. Everyone was gripped with great wonder and awe. I tried to figure out why he would do such a thing for me.

Tom boldly asked, 'Sir, we have seen amazing things today. What is your name and what does the nail represent?'

The man with the nail gently responded, 'My name is Jesus and this nail represents the price I paid for your freedom.'

I finally understood. The price he paid was dying on a cross for me. He took my place instead of me. I am no longer a slave. I was bought with a price, his life for mine. I now have my freedom. It was not a dream, but the reality of the transformation in my life when I met Jesus.

He has made all the difference in my life.

'Go around the entire world and tell them the good news of what I have done for you.'

+ + +

"So if the Son sets you free, you will be free indeed."
(John 8:36 NIV)

Prayer To Receive Salvation

Father God, forgive me for trying to run my own life.
I am sorry for the things I have done wrong and
I ask you to forgive me.
I confess with my mouth that Jesus is Lord,
and I believe in my heart that you raised Him from the dead.
Thank you that my past is forgiven.
Thank you for saving me.
Thank you for accepting me into your family.
In Jesus' name. Amen.

Thank you for reading my book. I'd love to hear your thoughts about it and whether you were encouraged. I would be very grateful if you would leave a review on Amazon.

All proceeds of the book sales will go to Global Care (globalcare.org). Global Care is a Christian charity helping vulnerable children that live in extreme poverty, all around the world. They give them access to life-changing education, working with local partners to transform their lives.

Printed in Great Britain
by Amazon